WESTALL '66

THE FINAL TRUTH

WRITTEN & ILLUSTRATED BY ERIK RINKEL

WESTALL '66: THE FINAL TRUTH

Printed in Australia by Amazon Kindle Direct Publishing

Published by Kaylon Press.

https://andrewharbisbooks.wixsite.com

ISBN: 9798711349600

ABOUT THE AUTHOR

Erik Rinkel has been an Arts educator and operative throughout his professional life. He has worked in Writing, Drama and Music Education at secondary and tertiary levels. Erik was a founding director of The Metropolitan Theatre and also of the Foundation, "ARTS 1000." He has written and performed in thirty-five radio plays for children, commissioned by the Singapore Broadcasting Corporation twelve children's books for Literacy teacher training in Sierra Leone, and a musical.

With grateful thanks to Anita, Zoë, Miki, Keenan and Andrew.

PROLOGUE

On April 6, 1966, an unidentifiable craft landed in some scrubland very close to Westall High School, in Westall, a suburb of Melbourne, Australia. The landing was witnessed by hundreds of students and teachers, but they were quickly and harshly informed that they were not to speak about this incident.

Not speaking does not mean not thinking, and I needed to structure an explanation for myself that the truth of all these people could be satisfied. Clearly they all saw something.

Some fifty-five years later, this book is my version of what happened that day if only I'd been allowed to speak.

I was there in 1966.

It almost doesn't matter what I saw anymore.

Or does it?

What matters is that, in an extreme situation, adults chose to behave badly because, in their eyes, children had no rights, not even the right to tell the truth.

In the absence of truth we need to wonder and create...

WESTALL '66 THE FINAL TRUTH

CHAPTER 1.
MAGNIFICENT

I WAS STANDING IN A massive, heavily ornamented chasm, approximately 4.88 Ok long by 39.23 Okts wide, with a ceiling height of exactly 200 Lesser Okts. I knew, from having been inside this space literally hundreds of times, that I was standing at the point called EDC—Exactly Dead Centre. That was my favourite spot, where you could see the most, hear the ultimate, and sense, well, the honest word. This was the place where the truth was spoken; where the truth had to be spoken.

But, to tell the truth, even though I knew exactly where I was standing, in reality I couldn't see, hear or sense a single thing. I mean, I can hear you wondering why I didn't just turn on a light. Good question. Ridiculous question. Good because it does seem logical, but ridiculous because there were no lights, not a single globe, pen torch, mobile phone, or even a struck match. Odd?

Well, why should there be, right in the most central middle of a black hole? And not any old shoe polish black hole lurking around common or garden galaxies. This was ULTERIATA BLACK HOLE GALAXY SUPERMASSIVATA.

Told you. And that's my home. Just to help you along a bit, all those measures and sizes of our meeting chasm, well that's how you would see things with your eyes, but in reality the whole chamber, hold your breath, was smaller than 1 billionth of an Okt. Wow, I hear you say. Yes, Wow I say right back at you, because that's what a black hole is all about, and only the mightiest, smartest and most powerful can survive there, and ULTERIATA is the most powerful of all!

My name is Prince Ek, the 74th and youngest son of King Ok and Queen Aggratenta, Supreme Beings of our beautiful ULTERIATA. Quite a burden having more than seventy brothers and sisters, all high achievers and, quite frankly, just a tad on the boring side.

Well, there's Tunata the Bedevilled, who single-mindedly took on the Massive Avalanche of Bedrock that accidentally roared into our universe while the hated Boron of Dul was sweeping his ultimate (not) star garden. Then sister Tunata, with one raised eyelid, heftily pushed back the many galaxies' worth of gigantic space rubble, thereby pleasing our parents no end. She was rewarded with a free trip to Heaven—which she hasn't cashed in yet.

There's also the annoying twins, Leo and Gem, who, yawn, excelled themselves by discovering the ruins of the old civilisation called INSEKTIVORUS ANTENNIII, a potentially rich and dominating community who made the mistake of eating everything within two hundred planets' reach of home and, when there wasn't a scrap of anything left, they devoured each other. What a find! Mum and Dad were just delighted with the twins' Kosmos shattering discovery, and they gave them Lifetime Membership of the Bravest Discoverers Club. What's worse is that Leo and Gem think that's something really special!

I'm a bit of an underachiever in everyone's eyes. Not quite a failure yet, although that could be just around the corner. I'm a bit nervous. I'm not sure what tonight's meeting is all about, but I did hear my mum speak the word Ek in an urgent and disappointed sort of way, and that's never a good sign.

And then it started. An astoundingly beautiful humming began in the most profound darkness. Notes rose, soared, dropped, hovered and splayed out in tangents of twenty, thirty maybe a hundred harmonies all at once, each adding to the incessant miracle of sound. The volume increased too, creating a sensation of millions of musicians, all at once subduing the tonal beauty to a simple hush, then powering the harmonies to levels of force that shook and rattled the walls. Millions of musicians. And there were. All in total darkness.

The concert wound down like a complicated rug design, with eventually just a few single notes, almost soundless.

There was an immense air of eager waiting among the shimmers of respect that I had only ever witnessed at the most serious Community Assemblies, and this certainly turned out to be one of those.

The Significant Ones entered, and a shining glow of curiosity flowed through the multitudes in anticipation. The Ultimate Supreme Being of Ulteriata, also known as King Ok—also known as Dad to seventy-four of us—stepped forward onto a pearlised stage that appeared suddenly from the darkness. For someone such as he, holding such a position of greatness, you'd expect a grand and magnificent being to be evident, I suspect.

In actual fact King Ok wasn't very tall, but a bit tubby, and he stooped forward somewhat. But did this matter one scrap of a nano atom? Not at all, for King Ok's magnificence came entirely from his voice, his penetrating, warm, thinking, meaningful voice that could all at once silence the concerns, fears and worries of everyone gathered at the Assembly. Everyone except me, that is, for have I not already mentioned that my name had, in earlier Grand Assemblies, been mentioned with some degree of worry? I stood in silence, trying hard to push out a loving and interested shimmer, while quietly wishing myself into something, somewhere, sometime else. The wishes were, sadly, pointless.

King Ok began to speak, and there was immediate and utter silence; a silence so peaceful and calming, safe and warm that every citizen could only feel uplifted and ready to listen deeply, meaningfully. They owed King Ok.

"Friends and fellow citizens. It is so very, very good to be with you all once again at our beloved Assembly, where all that matters, matters to all."

King Ok, Dad, Silver Tonsils, he did love meaningful statements like this, and he certainly knew how to play a crowd. There was severe nodding of Arms, and the occasional frantic flash of some extreme hue from an adoring citizen.

King Ok continued. "Citizens, fellow beings of worth. At these Assemblies I always have thousands of messages of great news and fortune to bring you all." A massive flourish of glowing agreement flashed through the Assembly. "But today, tragically,

I cannot. While many such messages do indeed exist, something so gross and painful has come to my attention that I honestly cannot speak of any good, knowing the tragic."

All at once, the cavern diminished into a semi being of dark grey. What was King Ok doing? What was this horror he spoke of? What did he know?

"Citizens, be attentive to my voice, and let the tons of love that I feel for you all flow through you. I will carry you all."

Such beautiful words these were, and indeed the multitude were calmed, although I did notice one member, my mother Queen Aggratenta, attempt to hide a most uncaring smirk. Even in the murkiest grey of the chasm I was conscious of this. King Ok carried on.

"Many, many, many zones ago of when Now Was Not Then Nor Will Be, we were the only living beings on this side of the line that divided Being and Unbeing. We were free to roam as we wished, so long as we never crossed this line. All this is our simple history, of course. Our travellers moved here and there, exploring exotic star formations, gliding down scintillating distant dust clouds, you name it. But then, and this was a one time event, a dreadful, unbelievable accident occurred. One of our most reliable tourist firms, Distant Sites, was involved in an accident, vile and unthinkable. As a result of some unprecedented shaping of new fragments of being in our outer space regions, the force of these realignments shoved our Distant Sites crew and their passengers across the line of Being and Unbeing, hurtling them amidst the most giant explosion that ever was, into new unmapped spaces filled with all manner of strange objects and life forms. They were flung beyond imagination into the very most distant darknesses, lost to us forever in the aftermath of this gigantic boom. Out of sheer terror we looked for a place of asylum, where we could be safe from the ravages of this new invading space. Fortunately, we were able to find this wonderful chasm where we could continue to exist. Our abilities to adapt to any circumstance saved us from the terrors outside. Our home may look like a black hole, but it is our support and our fertility. It is our hope. Then why am I so sad today?"

And at this he stepped to the side and motioned to a pathetic creature on his left, who might once have been one of us had the agonies of his experiences not left him an exhausted, wretched, whimpering wreck.

"Oh, King Ok," he said in a most gruesomely hoarse voice, "I have seen what none should see. Many Ultimate Lifetimes ago, I came upon a hideous blue-green little planet in my search for the Deeper Realities. I beamed my Thought Master down to the harsh base of this planet, and observed the ugliness of its inhabitants, inside and out. They were cruel, humourless, vain, self-seeking, grasping and dirty, but this was nothing compared to what else I discovered. It was on this planet that our tragic tour group run by Distant Sites, missing for 30,042 Okts and a half, now finds itself, on the now officially named Blue-Green Planet and in hiding, in a Giant Salt Liquid Pot, only to be hunted down by the citizens and consumed as some form of nutrition. The manner in which our friends and relatives were hunted down was horrible in the extreme. Their eight Arms of Brilliance, as we call them, were hacked away from their bodies. Those eight brains, our lesser thinking organs, lost all connection with each other and our Head Control. The whole mass of flesh, brain and deeper mind was then thrown onto a searing hot metal plate. Everything was subsequently chopped ruthlessly into small blocks and"—which is where the veteran began sobbing so uncontrollably from his most horrible memories that he could barely squeeze out his final word—"Eaten."

Now, in ULTERIATA BLACK HOLE GALAXY SUPER-MASSIVATA, uncontrollable sobbing was expressed, strangely enough, in total silence. The greater the silence, the greater the pain, and in this case the pain was so great that it almost, nearly almost, burst into screaming wails of agony. And so they stood, almost bursting at the thought of cruelties inflicted on their friends in a great salt pot, whatever that meant, in abject silence. In fact, so they stood for ages.

Which gives me the opportunity to backtrack a bit.

In some universes, they call us "Brilliant Flashes", and I can go with that. There are many, many gifted members of our world, and while I certainly don't pretend to be one of them, I do admire and respect them, unless they're my brothers and sisters, of course! In other smaller galaxies with duller citizens, they call us Ink Fish, simply because we can make whatever we want disappear simply by blowing our special Veil of Darkest Blue ink over them. Well, for goodness sake, nothing could be easier. You simply think the idea "Darkest Blue", and, gone, whatever! It's done! OK, personally I haven't mastered the art myself yet, but I'm onto it; any day now! Most important, though, is that I can be called an Oktopus, or, if I'm with my sister, we'd be arguing. No, just kidding, we'd be called Oktopi; a strong, beautiful word, but never say we have Tentacles, because we don't. We have "Arms". Arms, yes, Arms. Silly word really, if you say it two-hundred times, but there you go. Arms! And I certainly know no other being in the Vastest Eternity Of Ever And A Bit, that has Arms. And just quietly, I'm very proud of this fact: THEY'RE NOT TENTACLES!

So the community were still standing in grief, by the imagined salt pot far away on that nasty little Blue-Green Planet, when King Ok spoke again.

"Together we have felt the pains of our brothers and sisters. They live now in a bay of salty water, from which they are hauled and dragged in great numbers, only to be burned and torn apart in the name of food. Sustenance. How can anyone be sustained by slaughter? Upon hearing of this disgraceful and unthinkable treatment of our fellow beings, I, King Ok, have decided we must act, in great haste, and without question of how we operate this vital mission."

King Dad of Ok was at his best when he had a plan. This was bound to be a good one, I could tell!

"Queen Aggratenta, step forward. My beautiful Queen"—and I did think he went over the top a bit here because her face did look distinctly like a spurt of intergalactic lava—"you have heard of the agonies of our friends. I charge you, my dearest, with the task of travelling at once to the Blue-Green Planet, and bringing home to us every last one of our suffering dear ones."

Mum the Queen swept forward and stooped into a bow so deep, she nearly tumbled into a somersault. She quickly caught herself, softly crooning, "I shall do whatever you ask, oh Great One."

"But wait," said King Ok, "you shall lead the expedition and return a hero, no doubt, but you may not leave the Oktokraft for security purposes. You must remain on board. I have therefore allocated a Lieutenant to disembark from the craft and descend onto the planet."

Wow! My dad was such a sharp dude. Mum was more a princess than a Queen, so somebody else to do the hard yards was just the thing. And I could think of at least a thousand great contenders for the job.

"So, I have determined that your travelling companion, your Lieutenant will be …."

And here I craned forward to see every reaction ….

"…. That person will be Prince Ek, our Royal Son! Arise Prince Ek!"

CHAPTER 2.
MISSION UNBEARABLE

THIS WAS THE VERY WORST, the very most worst, the ultimate very most worsest moment I could ever have wished for. A hushed expectancy hung in the air, as the entire Assembly expected me to arise as instructed. Arise: so layered with weight and sophistication, what a way to put it. I could have coped better with a curt 'get up', or even an affected 'just pop up here for a sec'. But no, it had to be 'arise', as though I were some intergalactic warrior about to take his place next to the Sublime Ruler of All That Matters.

I arose as instructed, although I must admit I was probably a little on the slow side. I don't know what possessed me, but my mouth seemed to open without any effort, and out came the words, "Hi, Dad."

Out of nowhere, well actually out of everywhere, came those mocking sneers and sniggers that don't actually come from any noise, but you can hear them everywhere nevertheless. Beyond the silent mocking came the screeching vault noise of nasty disdain that only one member of the community could have made. It was my mum. I recoiled into my smallest self at this horror, conscious that now the whole Assembly would join in with her.

Miraculously, they didn't. Instead, my father, King Ok, stepped forward and said quietly and with great dignity,

"Hi, Ek."

At this, the finest arpeggios and cadenzas issued forth from the gathered multitude, producing sounds of such warmth and support that even Mum found it awkward to push out another shriek. She simply settled for an unpleasant smirk. My terrific dad, oh did I mention he was the King, spoke again.

"My son, Ek, my 74th child. I am sending you on a journey of great importance, which may involve much difficulty and even danger. As I explained earlier, many of our citizens are trapped on a grubby little planet far, far from here. Many have already perished from vicious and unthinkable deaths at the hands of the inhabitants of this planet. I have heard they are unspeakably ugly, rude and ill-mannered. It is your role, your given duty as a Prince of this Realm, to go at once to this bilious ball in space, and bring back our family and friends who are trapped in the Great Salt Liquid Pot. You, Prince Ek, will go to this place and make a difference. Go and psych yourself into The Royal Oktokraft waiting just beyond The Black Hole. Do not attempt to come home until you have succeeded. Your mother, the Most Royal Queen Aggratenta, will accompany you as your Most Royal Pilot. She is our Community's most travelled traveller, and she has even ventured to those regions beyond which no one must go. As a measure of safety, our Most Royal Queen Aggratenta must never leave the Kraft. You, Ek my son, must endure this task alone."

Now, that last bit was the hardest part of the task, since I seemed to have made quite a business out of the Art of Failing. Like when I accidentally made the Royal Stage tip over when I was trying to measure how many of me could lie on it. Unfortunately, my dad, King Ok, was also on it at the time, and my carelessness left him dangling from one little corner. There were at least five-hundred similar examples, but fortunately, I think, my dad chose to speak again. The terror inside me rose equally, again.

"Ek, your mother, the Fine and Gifted Queen Aggratenta, will not only escort you there personally, but she will also wait for you to complete the mission. The Royal Oktokraft will be moored on the dark side of that planet's moon, waiting. If the vile citizens of the Blue-Green Planet say things you don't understand, just tell them you're Dutch. I'm not sure what that is, or what that means, but through every Kosmos and Galaxy known to Education and The Arts, beings who are Dutch are always adored and cherished. Oh, and Ek, get this mission right. Don't let me down."

As if I wouldn't!

I bowed deeply to my father King Ok, to show him I would do my best, my most best, my ultimate bestest to bring our beloved citizens home, but I had the gravest fears that he might have chosen the wrong guy for the job, and a nasty snigger behind me told me there was definitely one other being who shared my doubts. Unfortunately, she was the very one I had to travel with.

And so I left The Vault with the perfect sounds of heroic music wishing great success. If only.

"Well look who's here lurking in the Royal Korridor, pathetically hiding in the shadows because he has no clue what to do next. Have you packed for our nice little holiday, Ek? No. Have you said good-bye to your father, Ek? Another no. Have you thought about your duties when we get to this forsaken planet, Ek? I think I can hear a further no. You know what, Ek? I think I could ask you another 32,784 nice friendly little questions, and for each one your answer would be no. NO! The word no. Oh, he who does not know! NO KNOW! Well that's so clever, I must remember it for along the way. Don't expect this to be a fun time, Ek. I know how useless you are. If your father thinks so little of me that it's fine for me to go on a major mission with a drop-kick failure and loser like you, then a few special measures are going to have to be put in place. See you on board, darling heart!"

CHAPTER 3.
THE JOURNEY

MUM REACHED THE DOCKING POINT way before I did. Well, she must have, because the whole of Zone Aquarius, which was entirely for her use and overwhelmingly huge, was piled to the Zenith with crates, cases, parcels and boxes. Goodness knows where she thought she was going, or how long she'd be away. In fact, I couldn't even see her, but I knew she'd be around somewhere because she'd never leave a precious stash unguarded. Inwardly I groaned, but I thought I'd better form a one-Oktoboy search party.

I began climbing the mountains of produce. Anyone would think her Oktokraft was about the size of The Great Vault, but it wasn't at all. Fortunately, Oktokrafts have no sense of size, weight or dimension, so you can just pack in whatever you want without limit. Since this was to be a mission of urgency, which I imagined to be like a flash strike, I could hardly imagine the need for these loads and loads of, well, what Mum might label 'necessities'.

I hadn't studied mountain climbing, but I imagined that to clamber across these thousands of parcels, laid out and up and across in the most haphazard patterns, far exceeded even the most challenging space mountain range. I could feel boxes slipping and actual contents snapping and breaking as I dragged myself through Mum's world. If this was just the packing stage, then what would the actual mission be like?

Just then, I slithered to the peak, glad that I was still in one piece myself. I spotted her way down below. She seemed to be sorting the parcels into colours, the cases into sounds and the boxes into feel sensitivity. She hadn't got to the crates yet because I was on top of them and I could see they were still unsourced. It was a time-old method of sorting things, and it always took aeons—aeons that we didn't have. Suddenly, as if she could smell something vile in her bizarre world, she snapped her whole body up in my direction, accompanied by a typically unpleasant snarl to introduce the flow of words that were about to come out.

"You! Fool! What do you think you're playing at? Haven't you noticed we're supposed to be leaving? You really just don't care about anything, do you?"

Luckily my temporary mountain built up my strength.

"Listen Mum, I've been wandering around searching for you, but I didn't realise you were moving house!"

Actually, I surprised myself with that moving house bit, and I couldn't stop giggling at the thought of how good it would be if she really did. I knew some really top space dwellings where she deserved to be.

Then, of course, the screeching started in classic style:

"Get down here now before I tell you what I really think! You idiot, clambering all over my possessions …!"

This was Mum's greatest performance gift, to rant and rave without breathing for at least 28 Okts!

"All right, Mum, hang on to whatever you've got left. I've arranged for twenty-five kind volunteers to help us get going, so sit back somewhere, and relax."

I pressed the Volunteer Lever on my Panel and, as I started sliding down the massive mountain of luggage, they entered the scene. Immediately Mum, who'd obviously had a bit of thinking time while I did my sliding, leaped up and addressed the helpers.

"Thank you, kind Volunteers, I appreciate your gracious gesture so very, very much. Now, as I will be this mission's Chief Pilot in Chief, I will be seated at the Main Konsole. Prince Ek here won't be needed until much later, if at all, so just place him at Konsole 2 next to the Emergency Exit. In fact, he should enter now, just so we know he's nice and comfy."

The Volunteer tribe lifted me all at once, carried me into the Oktokraft and placed me, with care and due gentleness, in front of Konsole 2.

"Don't forget his seatbelt, Volunteers," I heard Mum wail with glee, and I remembered, just when it clicked into place, that it was controlled by Konsole 1. My mother had locked me into the kiddie seat. I was trapped!

Of course, most of the luggage was placed right between the two Konsoles, so you-know-who wouldn't have to develop a migraine by looking at me. This was going to be some trip.

Everything was finally loaded, and Mum took her pride of place. In expected style, she activated the Soundboks, and her raspy voice became layered with a sugary sweetness as she spoke.

"Passengers all. I'd like to welcome you all on board Flight Oktokraft Royal bound for the Blue-Green Planet. We're expecting some smooth weather along the way, and our staff will go out of their way to meet your every need. We expect to be arriving at our destination in exactly 374 Okts. Enjoy your flight!"

"Yes that's hysterical, Mum, since it's just you and me and a bunch of boxes!"

"Aw, Diddy-Diddy, little boy's upset!" And with that word 'upset', she activated the engines and swooped magnificently towards our destination, gliding the Kraft effortlessly onto its long journey. She certainly knew how to fly.

'Oh well,' I thought. How much harm can she actually do on this flight? At least I've got an amazing view through the main window of the emergency door. I could really get into this.

But that was when the crackling of the Soundboks started up again.

"Dear passengers, we have a little boy on board with us today. Oh, he's a sweet little toddler, called Ekky-Ek-Ek, so I thought I might sing him this little song, especially dedicated to little people with little brains. Little kiddies shouldn't ever really truly fly. Haha! Just let them try! Here I go-oooo! And …

I'll take you through the airless sky, I'll take you to the careless sky

Oktobelt Oktobelt, I wanna keep you safe in your Oktobelt!

And with all due respect to the younger generations

Just keep your little brain on my REGULATIONS

"There you go, Ek, just for you. Now, here come the regulations:

1.   Don't speak to me. I can't stand the sound of your voice.

2.   I certainly don't want to speak to you.

3.   Whatever you think you'll be doing on this mission, forget it.

4.   You have no talents for this task, or any other.

5.   I'm in charge, and you're not.

6.   And never will be.

7.   You are nothing.

Now just look out the window like a good little chappie, ok?"

When you know someone is a ridiculous being, that's bad enough, but when that ridiculous being is holding you captive and saying dangerous, threatening things, then we have a coat of a different colour! The worst thing was that I'd never been able to figure out why I was the constant victim of this offensive rubbish. I wondered, with some hesitation, if I might try and figure out where things went so horribly wrong for her. I really couldn't figure out a point where I might have thought that I had brought all this rubbish on myself.

"You know, Mother," I said with as much quiet control as I could gather, "I just don't understand why you have to go to such great lengths to be so cruel and horrible. You just fling dirt whenever I'm in your neighbourhood. You throw barbs when you're only vaguely within throwing distance. I say this with all respect, Mum, but I think you're out of control."

A strange silence followed, throughout which I wasn't sure if she hadn't heard me, or if she was just quietly thinking about what I'd said, and maybe even that I was right in some small, pathetic way. I glanced down at the Konsole and noticed a plaque which bore the inscription, 'FOR PATHETIC BABIES ONLY!' I rested my head in my hands, feeling quite exhausted by the endlessness of this conflict. Almost at once, she returned with the vigour of a screeching space bird, a rare being known for the vicious and relentless hunting of its prey.

"Me? Me? I'm out of control? Look at you, you pathetic grain of space dust. You sit there fearful and pathetical, over by the Emergency Exit because you can't wait to get out."

"You told me to sit here, Mum."

"Oh, that's right. Everything's always my fault. Well, you know what? You're just stupid."

"I don't think so, Mum, I—"

"Shut up, stupid. I'm ashamed of you. There's nothing you do right. You have so many talented brothers and sisters who make me totally proud, but you, you just lurk around corners thinking, thinking what I ask you? Nothing, because you're just a stupid wastrel, and I can't bring myself to look at you."

There was a long silence.

"Shut up," she shouted from nowhere. You're just like your father, a massive disappointment. A failure."

A longer silence.

"And you know what, Ek?"

"What Mum?"

And what followed fell like the sledgehammer designed to cleave the Kosmos into minute splinters,

"You were a mistake."

You were a mistake.

A mistake.

I heard these words rolling around inside my head, like great thundering boulders of poison designed to crush me, forever.

"You were a mistake."

When I couldn't hold the agony of these words inside me any longer, the release came. One gasping great sob followed another, with barely enough breathing space in between to keep going. Each massive, choking sob came together with the word 'mistake', and I knew the echo of that would never leave me. Pathetic as I apparently already was, I remained in this painful, lonely state for I don't know how long. I felt as though I'd been in a massive accident, and I didn't know how I'd ever start to heal. I stayed immobilised, half lying over the Konsole, like I was in a strange coma in which I was aware of my surroundings and what had just happened. Then, although I felt nothing, I must have drifted off to an uneasy sleep.

I don't know how long, but when I did return to consciousness, I became aware of a very faint noise. I tried to locate its source, and when I eventually did, I realised it was coming from beyond the mound of boxes, in the direction of Mum's stronghold. An eerie sound it was, really, and it took me some time to realise she was sitting there, by herself, quietly weeping.

I was beyond knowing what to do.

CHAPTER 4.
GALAXY GAMES

I RETURNED TO GAZING OUT of the Emergency Exit window. These were parts of space I had not traveled through before, and I was struck by the extraordinary beauty I could see before me. First, we circled the widest field of ice I could ever have imagined, stretching from one extreme distant view to its furthest opposite. The ice was the whitest white, and right through this perfect, brilliant expanse there ran an unwavering, black line, cutting the ice field in two glorious semi-circles. I wondered who might live in this gleaming realm when, all at once, the massive white disc moved into a vertical wheel and rolled into deepest space. Almost at once, ribbons of gas and smoke danced in the space left by the ice field that had sped off in such an unexplained rush. The playful ribbons of gas twirled around each other, and flipped into exciting shapes and figures.

Just as soon as they had appeared, they vanished, making room for a field of thousands of stars, really quite of the diamond-like, yet regularly dotted with the darkest blue sapphire starlets. There were so many of these, and yet they seemed to glide effortlessly past each other. One classic structure followed another, floating past my vision, a cavalcade of performing artists like we some-times invited to come to The Vault back home. Strangely, what I have described to you was only the foreground of my view, for beyond these lay Kosmic Kloud formations, immense nebulas, spiralling galaxies storming towards each other, and there was even one space structure that looked like a tremendous key-hole, and I seriously did wonder what was on the other side.

Hope, perhaps. I didn't want to let my dad down.

A rasping voice took me away from my window watching.

"Ek, I'm going to stop for a bit at the Wayside Inn coming up, 'The Aurora Pastie Palace'. Love it. Sounds so royal. Like me."

Groan, you'd think that, with me being a Prince and her being my mum, she would know that I would already know she's Royal. See? This is what happens when somebody does your head in. Nothing makes sense. And a little voice inside said, 'And besides, I was a mistake anyway.'

"Can I come in too?" Of course I knew the answer already, but I thought I should at least try, if only to be annoying.

"Sorry, Ek, can't do. You're still tied into the Konsole, and there's no way I can get across all these boxes. I won't be an Okt."

Mum quickly zoomed into the Kraft-park of the Aurora Pastie Palace, just about falling over herself in the rush to get to the delicacies lurking inside this tacky looking wayside stop. And what was the rush anyway, since we were travelling in an Oktokraft stuffed full of delicacies from home. What was she thinking, ever?

She seemed to be inside forever, and it was rather tedious in the car park, since my only view was of a Black Star, whose only claim to fame was its total invisibility. Anyhow, Mum eventually emerged again, laden again of course.

"I'm back, and guess what I got, Ek!"

"Personality Powder?" I thought that was a light and fluffy joke, but clearly it wasn't.

"I've told you before, Ek, Shut up! You've wrecked this whole trip already just by being here. Don't embarrass me any more than you already do. Anyway"—and her voice took on that sticky honey tone again—"I've bought some lovely goodies! Let me just take off again and I'll tell you. Yummies!"

In the the flick of an arm, and sometimes I did actually think Mum had tentacles rather than Arms, she was back behind the wheel and we were surging through deep space again. Mum was clearly fixed by the demands of her duties.

"So, I bought Eclipse Cookies. You know, they're the ones you have to slide past each other on the way down as you eat them. Yum! Then I overstocked on Galaxy Lollypops. So good! Lots of Planet Crackers of course. They're a bit common but good as a filler, and everyone's favourite, Starry Night Juice. Can't go wrong there, Ek."

"What can I have?"

"Well, none of these, of course, there's hardly enough for one Oktopus. Hang on, you can have this," and she flung this little packet over the boxes, and of course it hit me in the face. It was a Colour-change Powder Pickle, and I can't even begin to describe the flavour. Even a machine would have spat it out. This particular type of Pickle had been designed on Planet Sulphura and ... do I really need to say more?

"Oh, good one Ek, I bring you a kind gift, and already I can tell it's not good enough. Just for once be grateful I got you anything at all. But you wouldn't even know what gratitude is. Thank God for the other children. You're a loser."

She had yet again worked herself up into such a venom bath, that she reeled the Oktokraft around dozens of the steepest, but imaginary corners. I was hurled against the Konsole, and I was bleeding quite rapidly, but I said nothing.

It was the safer option.

CHAPTER 5.
ACROSS THE LINE

AFTER AN UNNECESSARILY LONG SPATE of this temper tantrum hurtling, the Oktokraft began to settle on a more even course. I looked at the Konsole to confirm where we might be, but someone unpleasant had decided to program my data with lists of books for really small Oktobabies, such as 'Ek and the Very Grumpy Meteor,' and the old epic, 'The Day Queen Aggratenta Got Her Say,' and a whole lot more!

I turned off the Konsole, without even allowing myself to think about what I had just seen on it. Instead, I tried to calculate just how near we were to approaching The Kosmic Equator, where the qualities of certainty, precision and predictability no longer hold true, and everything is a huge guess. We had the great fortune to live with absolute certainty in our Black Hole; a certainty that had enabled us to build an immense world and a powerful and meaningful society. Of course, as you already realise, individuals might share some personal differences; I guess that's just the way of Oktopi. But not all Celestial Communities shared such fortune.

I apologise for this inky squirt of optimism. I'm just trying to cope.

Soon enough, The Kosmic Equator swung into sight. Strangely, I had expected this huge, deep and wide cliff, edged with the sharpest barbs of poison-laced rocks. I could sense the possibility of us being sucked into its depths or pierced by the barbs as the most agonising poisons dribbled into every smallest space in the Oktokraft. No such events! Instead, as soon as the Oktokraft crossed over the chasm of the Kosmic Equator, a total and quite perfect calm and peace descended over us. We glided quite smoothly across this endless sea of depth, and all I could do was to bathe in the sense of perfection it wafted up.

Here I felt safe, regardless of who else I was with.

After some time, and it was a beautiful length of peace, as the Oktokraft cruised through this stretch of space, I felt strong and revitalised. "Bring it on, whatever is still to come," I murmured to myself. And so I fell into a deep, nourishing sleep, carried on the shoulders of this generous and understanding Kosmic Equator.

I dreamed that I was back home with my father, King Ok.

"Ek! Ek! Wake up, you lousy good for nothing! Wake up now, I order you! Ek! Help me!"

It wasn't just the familiar screeching that yanked me out of my dream, it was also that the Oktokraft was bouncing, rocking around in a bit of a heavy way.

"Well, what would you like me to do, Mum? Will I read you the story of 'The Very Naughty Konsole?' You've locked me out, remember? I'm too useless to help. You're on your own, so here goes: 'Once upon a time, there was a very naughty Konsole called—'"

"Ek, no. We're in trouble here. You have no idea what's ahead."

"Oh sorry, Mum, I'm really into this story, '…naughty Konsole called Kitkit, and he had a very, very naughty plan—'"

"Ek please. I'll try and reconnect your Konsole. I can't do this alone."

There was a tone of extreme urgency in her voice, and I felt that maybe I owed it to my own commonsense to at least have a look.

"Ok, ok! So reactivate me then. This better be worth it."

"I'm nearly there, Ek. I just need to de-activate the Layer of Baby Konsoles. This should be it. Now press Effekt (())&&#677'lnil87*&(FwGgYFYJ-B."

Too easy!

Too scary!

The heavy, thudding, bumping continued, but I couldn't locate a cause for it. I tried to manoeuvre the Oktokraft away from this unknown source, but this was too difficult. Impossible in fact. Just as I was wondering when I would hear from Mum about my not fixing this problem soon enough, the Oktokraft lurched, not forward as you might imagine, but bolt upright, so through my window I could see the rarest point of all. There above me, unmistakably, I looked upon The Zenith, the highest and most central point of the known Kosmos. Well, I knew it was The Zenith because, just below it, there dangled a rare space sign, saying,

ZENITH! THE HIGHEST POINT EVER!

CAUTION!

SPACE TERRORS AHEAD!

HOW'S YOUR ZODIAC LOOKING FOR YOU?

Great, I thought, some space clown putting up threatening signs. That's all I need.

"Don't worry Mum, we're Cephalopods. We're not in this Zodiac yet. Pisces are, but who'd want to be one of them, eh?"

Mum didn't reply, which probably meant she was working out the many benefits of Oktopi compared to fish. Personally though, I couldn't help feeling worried by the little sign under The Zenith of all places.

The eternal calm of gliding in space is without equal. It's absolute perfection and, combined with the sleek smoothness of the Royal Oktokraft, ensured not only a safe, even passage, but also an inner sense of being at one with the abundance of the Kosmos. A splendid ideal.

But not for long.

Almost as soon as we glided away from the Kosmic Equator's almighty influence, small streams of alternative influences could be felt lapping against the Oktokraft's surface. Of course, the expected response wasn't long in the making, with,

"Ek! Ek! Do something. I think we're being attacked, Do something, you useless beast of burden!"

"Mother!" I was beyond calling her 'Mum'. Quite frankly. I realised I could never rely on her producing one fair character, with tools like consistency and niceness. "Mother, we're in deepest space. It's just a bit of bumpy weather. Just try and get a grip for once. Everything you come across is not some specially designed horror just for you to suffer. I'll do all the suffering for you. Does that make you feel happier?"

"Oh, for the sake of anyone who ever lived, just shut your unfortunate face, Ek, and ask yourself this basic question: why can't I be more like my mother? Just say this to yourself until I say stop, OK sweetie? Oh, and how was the pickle?"

Fortunately, I did not get the opportunity to reply to the stupidities thrown at me by my mother. I knew the space sign and its ominous warning could not be dismissed quite so easily as I had done, but what loomed now was proof that the sign was a reflection of what was to be, but exactly what was that?

The streams of gentle rocking lapping against the Oktokraft increased in energy. Gentle rocking became nudging, became pushing, heaving, bashing and forcefully tearing at the vehicle. We were clearly in the middle of a Solar Wind, although it soon became clear that we were nowhere near the middle as yet. More and more, the Oktokraft was lurched vast distances across this unknown expanse from all directions, tearing at the Kraft's outer protective materials. I could hear the straining of the Black Hall Fabrics, the very newest that had only recently been perfected and, while I had the utmost faith in their workmanship and strength, I just wasn't sure how much stronger this tearing wind could get.

This question was quickly answered for me when the blasting Solar Wind, now seemingly at its fiercest, was joined by an additional element; an immense, thundering slam of something against the Kraft almost knocked me out, as well as causing a massive landslide of Mother's goods. I couldn't tell where she was, and I was prevented from doing so by a continued barrage of meteors attacking us. Through the windows I could see their heavy enormity, but this did not make them slow or sluggish. They rammed at us with a vicious power, as though these rocks were equipped with minds to destroy aliens. Here, we certainly were aliens. The speed and force of the attacks doubled, trebled and more, when suddenly I remembered our only hope, a saying of my father's, "When in doubt, or in trouble, Ek, just turn everything off!"

I had never had the reason or opportunity to trial this philosophy, and King Ok was no stranger to making strange and even ridiculous statements, but in the middle of a Meteor Attack, who was I to question?

In a flash, I activated the 'ABORT ALL FUNCTIONS' lever. Straight away, the lever did what was asked, and everything went black; a profound black that was blacker even than a black hole. All I could feel was us going down, down, sinking into a safety way below the meteors. And the desperate speed of sinking felt almost like a warm blanket carrying us to safety.

Unfortunately, that wasn't the case. All lights and movement functions suddenly activated at tremendous speed. Before my humble window loomed an extraordinary Hyper-nova, an Ice Giant, And it was seemingly beyond control, suffering from wild twisting and hurtling blindly through space. I levered the Oktokraft upwards to try and roll over the Ice Giant and escape its wild quivering. After an eternity of trying to keep up the vertical flight, and another of just wishing we'd survive this, I knew we were freed from this strange, enormous monster, when the ice lands of this giant slipped away below my vision.

Predictably, of course, a new wonder took its place. Exhausted from what I'd been through so far, and not having any idea where Mother was, I wasn't at all ready for the next scene that approached me. It was a set of seven massive planets, all identical in a glowing red. They were in a formation of an amazing kind. Planets 1, 3, 5 and 7 were in a line, across what looked like the 'top'. Way below them, and between, was the row of Planets 2, 4 and 6. This remarkable formation enabled the two rows to swap places, with the top row planets sinking to the bottom, and the bottom row rising to the top, endlessly, ceaselessly, like a massive machine chomping its way through space. And of course they were headed straight for us. The whole structure was already too close to escape from, either up or down. This left only one choice. With gritted teeth, I headed straight for those gaps between the red hot rotating planetary wheels. Searing temperatures were recorded by the instruments, all the while rising, rising as we surged right through the middle planets. Without warning or explanation, the seven giant balls split off, at breakneck speed, and stopped at some huge distance beyond. I watched them, apparently preparing for a return regrouping, so with great haste I forced us out of this terror zone.

Distant waves of heat, and wind, and ice, and fragments of rock still accompanied the Oktokraft, but I finally had the feeling that we might be through the worst of it. And after another massive sweep of all the accompanying debris, there it was, right in front of me.

The Blue-Green Planet.

CHAPTER 6.
LANDING

"MOTHER! MOTHER WHERE ARE YOU? I haven't got time for this sort of nonsense."

This actually felt like a pretty silly thing to say. Not having time didn't mean much when I was hurtling through alien space towards an unknown ball in the distance. Would the inhabitants there even have time, or know the concept of time? So where was Mother then? And what was the time?

I realised that a bonus of all that I'd just been through, along with my dad's wise advice to turn everything off, was the seatbelt that kept me trapped in the Royal Baby-seat. Without the slightest effort, it sprung open to give me access to a renewed freedom.

"All right Mother. Do I believe you're so ridiculous you'd play control games at this point? Yes, probably. But just on the one percent miniscule chance that you're not, I'll have one of those quick as a flash searches. Just to make matters easier, try and stay wherever you are now."

I moved as fast as I could among the heaps of boxes and things that had all been tossed about, many broken during the journey. But that was not the main priority. Searching for Mother was strenuous, what with the mountains of debris I had to slip through, as well as frustrating, because I really had no idea where to look, and ultimately annoying because I could not forgive the words she had said to me. Nor could I undo them.

I spotted the tip of an 'Arm' some metres away, which I recognised as being Mother's because it held the Royal Seal Ring on it. The rest of her was evidently buried under a deluge of her own greed. Like a flash, I pounced towards her, and frantically scrabbled around the rubbish to locate the rest of her body. Every food texture was represented in the mass that covered her, but around her face area she was smeared in a mixture of sickeningly slimy and severely sticky deposits. She looked like she was wearing the whole Wayside Stop. My mother the lowly shop. I tried to wipe some off just to restore some of her dignity, when one of my Arms slipped on the slime and lodged itself in one of her nostrils, and gripped hard, thanks to the stickiness. And, of course, this was when she woke up.

"Ek! Get that thing out! You useless being! I knew you'd try to assassinate me one day! You nasty creep. Suffocation by blocking the nasal passages! You wait till I tell King Ok about this, now get me up, dead-head!"

She really wasn't in much of a situation to get up. She was weighed down by all the gunk she had acquired, and she had pretty much been bashed about by the Kosmic Storms we had endured. In fact, she looked like a bit of a wreck.

"You lie down, Mother, and see if you can quietly clean yourself up a bit. You've got stuff to do later. Right now, I'll get us down to the Blue-Green Planet and its Giant Salt Liquid Pot."

Quick as a flash, I lunged towards Konsole 1 and locked myself in. What a feeling. Behind me I could hear the scrapings of stink and slime. Some temporary justice at least, but not the kind that leaves you, well, full inside.

"You engineered this, you little imbecile." Sometimes words like imbecile seemed like the kinder ones.

Nevertheless, the prevailing winds were still shearing across the bow of the Oktokraft, and the path towards the little planet was not exactly safe and secure. Of course, it didn't help that I had no idea where the Giant Salt Liquid Pot was, or even what it was! Where was I to look? And those cursed winds from the sides just wouldn't let up. I tried a few knobs on the Konsole in the hope of some directions or a map, but it was no use. Mother had been such a seasoned traveller all her life that she didn't need maps or notes. She just knew where she was going. Well, I didn't, and I had to make the best of a bad lot. And besides, those pesky winds seemed to be making the decision for me. Closer and closer we sped, and still I had no clues about Salt Pots. As we entered the planet's atmosphere, the Oktokraft detected the presence of a large body below, and began a rapid slowing down according to its presets. Down and down and down we glided, when I realised I'd better look for a suitable landing site. I could see endless large solid structures, so I didn't want to take a chance of landing on these. Then, behind what seemed like an extra large structure, I spotted an open space. I pointed the Landing Finder in its direction, and quite calmly we floated down.

"We're in the wrong place, Thick Head!" Mother was standing right behind me.

"I had no choice. I had to land here. I've got to get out fast,

Mother. Look! There are aliens running towards the Oktokraft. Here, I'll take the panel from the Konsole. You won't need it. You know where you're going, and it's only to the back of this planet's moon. I'll leave by the Emergency Exit."

"Remember, you're plugged in as Dutch, whatever that is. One of your father's meaningless ideas. It's a new program, so there might be some glitches."

I hung the panel around my neck. "I've got to get out of here fast! The aliens are coming!"

I opened the E.E. door, and slipped out. It wasn't as easy as I had expected because the panel was way too big for hanging around my neck, and I was nearly decapitated as I slid out the Oktokraft. It would, I hoped, continue feeding information whether it was around my neck or not. I realised I'd have to abort this tool for my own safety, so I took it off and slipped it under some dirt where I might find it later. Hearing the sounds of the approaching aliens, I ran in the opposite direction to get away, and to give me some thinking time.

And to temporarily reflect on the thought that, although I was lost on an alien planet, I was free from my mother.

And also I was Dutch, whatever that was.

CHAPTER 7.
SCHOOL

AS I MOVED AWAY FROM the landing site, I felt pretty confident that I'd be able to retrieve the panel some time in the future. I started to move swiftly, darting out of the open space where the Oktokraft was still stationed, and towards, well, I wasn't too sure. Despite basically being lost, and who wouldn't be, one brief moment after landing on an alien planet, I had a sense of well-being and the profound sensation that things might be OK—a bit.

So I ran, and the more I ran, the more I became aware that I was running considerably faster than I was at the start. I glanced down and noticed my eight Arms had been replaced by two long gangly things with blocks on the end. These extensions were particularly ugly, but I certainly managed to move much faster than on my own time-worn Arms, so I decided to just count my blessings. Along the way, I noticed signs sprinkled here and there; it's a well-known fact that space travellers will recognise and be able to read signs as a matter of Intergalactic Courtesy. These ones said 'Osborne', 'Westall' and 'Rosebank', and frankly they sounded about as much like Mother's doubtful delicacies as anything else. I raced on until I came to a fenced clearing, which was next to a huge metal structure with giant metal ropes attached. I could feel a strange vibration coming from this object, and I rushed to get away from its nasty energies.

I turned and ran towards the site of the many aliens. They all had their backs to me and were clearly fixed on where the Oktokraft had landed. I stood as close behind as I dared. Almost imperceptibly, the Oktokraft rose slowly into the air, with Captain Mother in charge. Then, with the blink of my eyes—two new alien eyes as it happens—the Oktokraft veered into the distance, and vanished almost at once.

"To the back of the Moon," I murmured to myself, and I felt a bit alone.

Suddenly, the alien right in front of me turned around quite abruptly.

"Oh, hello. I didn't mean to startle you. Who are you?"

"Hello. I'm Ek and I'm Dutch," I replied enthusiastically, "I'm new today."

"I'm Mr Gently, and I'm a teacher here. I'm a bit distracted, because I think I lost my camera. But never mind, it'll turn up. I'd lose my head if it wasn't screwed on."

I was a bit concerned that these aliens screwed their heads on, but this man seemed incredibly warm and welcoming by unknowingly informing me that I was in a school.

"It's all a bit confusing here today, Ek, because this strange flying craft landed just there in The Grange, and then took off with a speed no one's ever seen. It does raise a few questions. Did you see it, Ek?"

"Mr Gently, I think I saw it land, but I really didn't look around too much. I'm already struggling with the idea that this place looks nothing like Amsterdam." Amsterdam: another one of those Panel words that I didn't have a clue about.

"Amsterdam?" said Mr Gently excitedly, "I've been there! Where did you live?"

Come on, Panel, process this one fast! "Opposite the Oosterpark."

"Beautiful! I know it well. Now I think I'd better find you a few friends, Ek. Let me see. Actually, you can't go wrong here. These are some of the most spectacular kids that I've ever met."

Mr Gently walked a few steps towards a group of friends. "Bobby, look what I found for you all to welcome to the school."

"You're a new kid, aren't you?"

"How did you know that?" I asked, more with curiosity than courage.

"I didn't, but you've got that daggy new kid look! I'm Bobby, pretty much the school brain."

Another one swung around, and quickly added, "More like the school clown! So, new boy, the clown is Bobby, I'm Kayleen, and you are …?" She sort of left the question dangling in mid-air.

"I'm Ek Van Ok," I announced. I realised by their reactions that the distant Panel in the dirt seemed to know what it was doing, even if I didn't. I must've looked like something they were familiar with—a genuine citizen of Blue-Green Planet.

Kayleen continued, "So, Ek Van Ok, do you wear clogs?"

Immediately I blurted out, "Well, of course I do. Sometimes our travel demands a bilateral correlation of the time fraction. So yes, that's what we do."

I could tell by the gobsmacked look on Kayleen's face that perhaps the Panel had been a little over-enthusiastic, so I laughed and said, "Gotcha! That was from a film I saw back home."

"Yeah, I get it; I think I saw that same film." Then she shouted at the others in her pack, "Hey guys, here's a new kid, Ek Van Ok. He's Dutch, but I can't see any clogs." She laughed generously, as though I was missing some kind of huge joke, which I obviously was.

Another of the group approached, taller than the others and quite serious in outlook.

"I'm Con. Con Papachristodoulopoulos, but that's a bit long, so you can just call me Papachristodoulopoulos for short."

"Well, that's a relief," I offered. "Where did that man go, Mr Gently? He was so helpful when I walked in. I just wanted to thank him."

"That's typical Mr Gently," replied Con, "he's always there when you need him, then when the problem's solved, you can't see him for dust. He's the best, Ek. Anyway, did you see the space ship?" Con asked, with a mixture of concern and interest.

"Yes, sure did. I didn't realise what I was seeing, but that was it. So fast! It's not something Dutch people travel in, that's for sure."

"Yeah, Greeks don't either. I wonder where they were from? Or where they're going?"

""Maybe we'll never know," I replied, desperately trying to sound wise. Fortunately, another of them interrupted.

"Ek, I'm Sheila. Sheila Nutter, and I don't get it." She hesitated, her face revealing a thinly veiled dishonesty. "There's just something about you. I'm not sure. We'll just see, eh?"

And in return I thought, 'I think I'll have to watch my step around you.'

But out loud I said, "What a strange thing to say to a stranger. I think maybe it was you who fell out of that space ship!"

The others heard that wise-crack and pretty much doubled up with hysterical laughter. Sheila was clearly not moved, and she continued to glare at me like she'd just eaten twenty or so of those famous space pickles I told you about. Of course, difficult questions continued to be thrown my way, and I did my best to answer them. Mostly everybody laughed and thought I was OK, except for Sheila Nutter, who really was a main worry, and therefore a danger to the whole mission.

Everyone was finally in agreement that the spaceship was not going to come back, or even do a glory tour in a circle around this school. It was gone, and probably connected to its berth at the back of the moon by now.

Con asked, "Hey Ek, do you know what class you're in yet?" I shook my head, not really understanding the question. What class? At home I was a Prince; a part of the Royal class. How could he know?

"It's fine, Ek, don't look so worried. Just come with us. We'll look after you. There's always a spare seat in our class, and most of the teachers won't even notice. Let's go! LET'S GO!"

He seemed to understand, but of course he couldn't. He was just kind, without trying to find out why he needed to be. At Con's loud command to move to class, the whole group started running towards the buildings. They all seemed to know exactly what was going on, so I just followed. One thing though—and I don't really want to say this because, apart from Sheila Nutter, everyone was so welcoming—although these Blue-Green Planet dwellers seemed so physically ugly and grotesque that it was sometimes hard to look at them. And to think that I had become of the same shape and features was certainly on the distasteful side. I feared a reflection, that was for certain.

While there was distinct movement from the whole crowd who had witnessed my landing and Mother's departure, the mood was not at all casual. There was a distinct hammering of important questions that everyone wanted answers to. This was clearly not a regular event, having flying saucers fall out of the sky. And why? Why Earth, and why this place that they called Westall? It seemed that pockets of uncertainty were developing among the crowd. I felt sorry that I had created this, but I was hardly in a position to get up in front of everyone to tell them everything was fine and the upheaval was just me landing my Oktokraft. That would jeopardise my purpose for being here and probably cause much unwanted fear. For now, I was destined to play along.

"Come on Ek, this is our room," said Con. "We'll sit at the front. Offence is the best defence. I tell you, nobody will even notice you're a newby-newboy."

"Wow, Con, that offence bit. That's so cool. Groovy!" Quietly I thought, 'Oh come on Panel, get it together! And where did "groovy" come from?'

Con leaped, like a gazelle, to the front seats of the middle row. I had my doubts about this full frontal seat, but as I was rapidly learning, what did I know? Just then, a large version of the aliens entered the room.

"Good morning, everyone, or should I say, Selamat Pagi. Selamat Pagi everybody. And what do we have here, right before my very eyes? Are you a new student in our Form One class? I'm Mrs Lorelei and it's so very nice—"

Just as I was growing purple with embarrassment, good old Con sprang to the rescue.

"Mrs Lorelei, what are you saying? Don't tell me you've forgotten. This is Ek Van Ok, and he started last week. Hey guys, when did Ek here, next to me, start in this class again?"

Of course, they all said at once, with great precision, "Last week, Con!"

"See, Mrs Lorelei. Didn't you put his name in your book? I hope you didn't forget. It's not like you to forget."

Mrs Lorelei delved into her book, and indeed, it appeared she had forgotten. "Ah yes, here he is, right here in my book," she said, to save face the way teachers always do.

I took a really long look at this Blue-Greener. So far she was clearly the least fortunate to look at and to be in the presence of. She had wrapped herself in one of those hairy coats that are available cheaply in all galaxies, and frequently likened to the constellation Ursa Major, the Greater She-Bear, and this was how Mrs Lorelei was now printed in my mind. She was also a dill. In my world, only the cleverest citizens could become teachers, but here was living proof that this was not so. Then I thought, what if she is such a clever operator that she keeps her brilliance hidden? Very well hidden, in fact?

It's hard with new people in your life. You're not sure if they're likeable or devious or shy or empty vessels or whatever. It seemed that now, in this new world, there were so many to meet, and I couldn't afford any mistakes.

Mrs Lorelei went to the board at the front of the room and picked up a very small white stick, which enabled her to write.

'Please, Panel, please be on track now. I think I need help,' I thought. When would the Panel be fully loaded and charged so I could at least feel secure in what I was saying?

Fortunately, it was prepared for me, and I was able to read the white script. She had written the words 'ini' and 'itu'.

"'Ini' and 'itu'; the two most important words in Indonesian."
Everyone nodded, smilingly. So far so good, until Con leaned
over to tell me,

"We've been back at school for six weeks now, and every single
Indonesian lesson she's done nothing but this 'ini' and 'itu'."

"Now children, I hope this is not too hard for you, but 'ini'
means 'this', and 'itu' means 'that'. Is that too difficult?"

There was a mixture of replies, like "no Mrs Lorelei" or "way
too hard for me" and "I love this stuff!"

I knew Con could see what I was thinking, but he signalled to
me to keep my mouth shut.

"Ek, listen, there's a lot of stuff going down at this place. Again
today with the space landing. When Mrs Lorelei does her 'ini'
and 'itu' lessons, it gives us a chance to talk and to figure out
what's happening. Sometimes I wonder if Mrs Lorelei does
this on purpose, to give us a bit of space."

Con turned around and spoke to Willy, who was sitting behind
us. "Willy, this is Ek, he's new today. This is Willy, Ek."

But Willy didn't speak.

"Willy never speaks," said Con. "Some people call him Silly
Willy because, somewhere along the line, he got locked inside
himself. He's the best kid. Nobody'd better try and hurt him.
He tried so hard to cope with everything going on, but one day
he just stood in the schoolyard completely lost, and he didn't

know where he was. He keeps turning up every day, but he doesn't get any of it. He just stares from one person to the next. And you know what? He's probably the nicest person in this whole place."

"I can see that, Con," and inside I felt this rage begin to well up.

"Life's like that, Ek. We all have a reason for who we are and why we're here. Like I said, life's like that."

I looked at Con and wondered what could have brought him down like that. 'Life's like that,' he'd said. Over my dead body! And maybe it wasn't my business to know all the details, as long as I could do something to help the effects.'

Meanwhile, the classmates were fully into their discussions about the flying thing that had fallen from the sky. They were, quite naturally, very eager to learn more, but for the moment they had to be content with just chatting.

A noise rang throughout the school, signalling it was time for the next lesson. Mrs Lorelei sank deeper into her bear coat and picked up her vital record book. She stepped towards me.

"Well Ek, I hope that wasn't too difficult for you. Have you ever done Indonesian before?" To which I replied, "Saya pikir hari ini saya belajar sebanyak anda."

She looked clearly flattered. "Well now, who's the clever one?"

"Indeed," I replied.

With no particular instruction, the class drained out of the classroom and into the corridor. For no apparent reason, the girls found it necessary to veer to the left, while the boys opted for the right. I don't know where the girls went or what motivated their sudden migration, but the boys headed for the back of another building where there was more spiky green stuff, just like I had encountered on my run from the Oktokraft. In all honesty, I felt quite good about being here. On the whole I had been welcomed warmly, except by the Nutter, and nothing too awful had happened as yet.

That's when Mr Stipple entered the scene. Even with my very short Blue-Green experience, I could tell he was a tense, self-opinionated slob, and a peasant doused in a whole range of ignorance. Oh, we had these at home too, of course, but these were quickly dealt with to work on the Fire Giants, until they could show publicly that they had learned how to cool themselves down. I must say, though, that I did fear a bit for Mr Stipple's chances.

"So here we are again, everyone. P.E. Now I know the term's been going for six weeks, but I can't in all honesty remember you lot at all. This is not a great impression, because it probably means you're all useless and pointless. Now, when I was at school, everybody loved P.E. best. We worked hard at it until we were the best, the best in the world. As you probably know, I've been a very famous League Footballer, and from there I entered the Olympic Games in Rome. I've had a lifetime of success and fame, and that's why I, Ted Stipple, have come here to Westall High School, to devote myself to you sad cases who don't give a hoot."

"Aha!" A location clue. That should help, for no reason other than to work out where I am, in relation to the Giant Salt Liquid Pot.

"Now you, Sunshine, who looks like he's got zero interest in all this, any questions from your advanced mind?"

That 'Sunshne' was me he meant, so I had to think quickly. "Um, P.E. Where I come from, called Dutch, P.E. translated means Precalculus Education. It helps us to distinguish between trigonometry and algebra, of course."

Someone kicked me from behind. "Don't be a smart-arse, Ek. It doesn't go down too well with some of the teachers. Especially this reject."

"Well then, Mr Precalculus, thanks to the little professor here you can all do some of the most horrendously painful exercises in the world, except for that place called Dutch, whatever that is."

"Sir, sir!" Con suddenly sprang to his feet, "Could you just tell us which League Football Team you played for?"

" Well, you've got to understand things were a bit different then—"

"Yeah, but football is football."

"Well it's a bit hard … ."

Just name the place, sheesh!

"Cooladdi," he mumbled quietly.

"Cooladdi, Queensland? Population Minus forty-seven and a half? We did that in Geography with Mrs Boundry. That's about the smallest place in the country. No wonder you got on the team! And what did you do in the Olympics?"

"That was really spectacular. I was umpire for the Marbles."

Huge mocking laughter rang out, and Stipple realised that he had made his position worse.

"That's it! That's it, you mongrels! You don't know real achievement when you're looking at it. Right, on your feet. Exercise one, and if it's not brilliant you'd better be ready for something really painful still to come. Right Lunge Jumps, which means you have to move at least five metres at each jump. You son, yes you, Silly Willy, you can go first. Jump, Stupid Wupid!"

I could see Con's face screw up in a spiral of barely controlled anger. His blood had drained from every particle of his eyes and face. I leaned over to him and whispered,

"Con! Just hang in there. Your time will come. Come on, breathe."

Willie tried with all his might, but he could only propel himself the smallest distance forward. Mr Stipple moved up to him, right in his face, and globules of saliva were building up ready for the onslaught.

"What's wrong with you, you useless piece of excrement? What sort of a spastic are you, Silly"—and he delayed here for a few seconds just to drag out the agony—"Willy?"

There was complete silence. The horror of Stipple's outburst had escaped nobody. Things had to change. Silly Willy would be Silly Willy no more!

"William," said Con, "come and stand by me for a bit. Dry your tears, because this teacher might well need your hankie soon. And Mr Tipple, could I just point out to you that, at the end of our last lesson, when you called William something equally disgusting which rhymes with 'bird', we followed you out of the school to the back of Humes Pipes, where you started smoking something that smelt heaps like marijuana, and I should know because my uncle in Orange grows it. And then that made me wonder what I could do with this knowledge if you acted like an outspoken thicko one more time."

"Correct! Now, that's Precalculus," I added, just from the joy of being on the side of a winner.

"Hey, Mr Stipple! I like your shoes. Is that raccoon fur?" Con added.

"Shut your cake-hole, sonny, or you might end up in a lot of trouble." Classic Mr Stipple.

Unstoppable Bobby heard a cue for his entrance, "Cake-hole!" He absolutely screamed with laughter, "Cake-hole? Whoever says cake-hole? Is there a bread-hole, or a cream-bun-hole? Hey, I know! A sausage-roll-hole." Pretty soon the whole group of students were rolling on the green stuff, laughing until they couldn't take any more.

With a stiff air of control, Mr Glass, the Principal, chose to breeze past.

"Everything OK, Mr Stipple?"

"Oh um, yes thank you, Mr Glass." He looked around frantically, flailing his arms, desperate for some explanation for this riot in the making. "This is my favourite class, and we're just doing some Laughter Exercises; they're recommended by the U.S. Marines."

"That sounds most commendable, Mr Stipple. Good work."

"That's right, Mr Glass, they're very helpful for the satisfactory expulsion of matter from the Intestinum Crassus," piped up Con.

Mr Glass smiled a thin smile, which was most generous for him, "Well, it's great to see a class in thinking mode, especially after all that space junk ballyhoo nonsense. What a palaver! What a papaya! I'll be nipping all that in the bud, you wait and see."

"Thank you, Mr Glass," Stipple said for no particular reason.

"While you pass the joint around, Stipple," added Bobby in his most disguised voice. Naturally, this caused more laughter of that uncontrollable kind.

"I see you're back to those exercises again," Glass offered, "enjoy!"

As he left, Stipple looked around wildly. "What did you say to Mr Glass? That funny foreign talk. What did it mean?"

"It means he'd benefit from a giant poo," said Con, without humour.

I can't in all honesty say that any of this sort of conversation bore a likeness to the learning we have at home. Nevertheless, I was curious to see how it all blended to achieve a particular purpose. Even though these kids were under threat from a pretty vile alien, they held their own, like a strong brotherhood. Parts of me were beginning to feel happy to be here, although I knew I was still lacking in the skills department.

The group walked back to the main building in the best of spirits and entered Room 13. This was a class worth waiting for; the special highlight of every day, except Wednesdays, when they had double Stipple instead. Afterwards, they had Science, the subject they looked forward to most.

Back in the room, everyone chatted busily and noisily about all that had happened so far that day. It had been an epic day, and good on Con, and good on Bobby and good on—SLAM! The door slid open with way less resistance than the opener had expected. Of course, it was Umame Bonn, late, but always relied upon for a major return entrance.

"I'm back," she shouted enthusiastically, as if no one had noticed.

"Umame, it's nearly lunchtime, where on earth have you been?" And this was followed by about twelve questions all meaning the same thing.

"Well, I haven't been to the movies, and I haven't been to the dentist, and I haven't been to one of those pushy Brighton Girls' Schools to pick up my first fat scholarship cheque, and more. In other words, can't tell you; bad luck, too slow!"

"Who cares anyway, Umame. You're such a sad case," piped up Bobby.

You could clearly see that Umame and Bobby were old friends by the easy way they treated each other.

Bobby persisted, "Umame, I've got someone to meet you. It's Ek Van Ok. New boyyyyyyy."

"Hi Umame," I offered, unsure of what I would get in return, but she was already ten topics ahead, only managing a quick greeting between what was on special in Coles, and gossip on the Form 2 kids.

"Well, I ran into Trev and Jude on my way into school, and they're already talking action. Glass has been ranting around the school carefully picking his enemies. He's out to kill, and all I know is that his main target is Mr Gently."

And the familiar glide of the metal door told us Science was about to start.

There was absolute silence. Extreme silence. A man with thick black spectacles and a hundred books came into the room. Quietly he said, "Sit down, please, everyone."

And, as everyone slid into their seats, he smiled as he spotted me in my front-row seat.

"Hello again, Ek, how's it all going?"

"Great thanks, Mr Gently. Things are certainly different here."

"You're lucky you speak such terrific English. You've got to watch out for some of these characters though, they're always trying to play jokes. Anyway, you've certainly picked a good day for arriving, Ek, what with the landing of the space ship."

I laughed at his jollity, "That's right, only I didn't land in the back yard myself. My spacecraft was called 'KLM-ROYAL DUTCH AIRLINES'."

(Thanks again, Panel. No further contact required from here on I think. I'm on a roll.)

"Some people think I've stepped out of a space ship, just because I'm a scientist. But you know what, Ek? Scientists are supposed to have wacky ideas; otherwise we wouldn't learn anything. Now Ek, as I said before, if there's anything you need, just come and ask me. I live in Room 17 most of the time."

Mr Gently then spoke to the whole group. "Things have been a bit different from usual." He turned to William and said, "Come and sit closer, William, at the front, between Ek and Con maybe." And William walked with a calm dignity to his newly allocated place. Clearly he didn't always giggle like he was out of control.

"This morning, before recess," Mr Gently started, "some Form 2 students came running to me, saying they had seen a flying saucer in the sky. Some of them were hysterical, screaming in disbelief at what they'd just seen. And, apparently, it was still there, in the sky. Quick as a flash, I grabbed my camera and started taking photos. It was just as they had described. Unbelievable in so many ways, and right here at Westall High School! The craft then headed towards The Grange. In the crush of things, my camera must have slid from my shoulders. I looked for ages. That was my physical, scientific evidence and I lost it. The thing is, there were students there who saw my camera being taken off my shoulders by someone behind me, but they couldn't identify who it was because the crowd surging towards The Grange was too thick. Of course, some people are really angry now. Be careful what you say around the school. That camera was my real evidence. It's likely and possible, I guess, that countless spacecraft have visited our The Earth for thousands of years, but I say again, the camera was evidence, and I'm a scientist." Everyone nodded deeply, out of respect. Inside they were thinking, 'Definitely an alien spaceship, evidence or not.'

I found that I had to agree, given my arrival. And besides, if so many of these students saw the Oktokraft, wasn't that a type of evidence too? I found it odd that one pair of hands could undo this evidence of hundreds—what a strange planet.

"Now then," continued the amazing Mr Gently, "does anyone have a question they'd like to ask me?"

There was a lot of thinking and wondering about the 'Do you

have questions?' question. Then Umame put up her hand, with an excruciatingly serious look on her face.

"Mr Gently, do you think Bobby is an alien?" And the whole class burst out in shrieks of laughter at that very definite possibility. In the middle of all this, I was beginning to feel that maybe I could belong here.

"Oh my goodness, Umame, what a frightening thought. Imagine what all the real aliens would think. But now, I can see nobody wants to do any work, least of all me. So William, to the cupboard please." On command, William walked to the front cupboard that had signs 'BORING BEAKERS' and 'PATHETIC PIPETTES' glued to it. He opened the door and produced what I realised was a musical instrument, although I had never come across one like this before. William sat down with the instrument; he tweaked a few gleaming knobs at the end of a long bit, and waited.

Mr Gently said, "Music Time; because Music is a Science too, you know. OK William, do you know the Dreamer song? Right then. I don't think the writer meant it to be sung in a Science Lab, but anyway—hit it Fingers William!"

And they played, and they sang, and William strummed. Now, it may not have been as musically perfect as my earlier childhood had taught me to expect, but there was a different perfection here. As I scanned from child to teacher, I saw such exchanges of genuine affection and loyalty that went way beyond the precision of the musical notes. It was a deep, long-term trust that made me somehow, well, a bit envious; it's odd how a sense of loneliness can creep into the happiest of times. I didn't want to give into it, so I listened to the words of the song:

Young eyes of the new world

Lay down the days of old

Claim back your dreams of gold

Gentle dreamer

Take my hand and hold it tight

See the white bird lead the flight

With your friends you know it's right

To be that......

Gentle dreamer

I was told later that not every class in every school would have wanted to sing that song today. They were too upset and confused about everything that had happened earlier. But here, in this odd place called Westall High School, this group of kids and their one adult made a connection that turned dorky into desirable.

Not like me and my mum. We put the 'd' in despicable.

The lesson ended and we all left for lunch. On the way out, Umame suddenly squeezed my hand for just a couple of counts. She let go, saying, "As the song says, Ek!"

"Thanks," I said, feeling excessively shy. "Hey Umame, you're like a butterfly. You fly in and out, just helping."

"I know, Ek, we've all got a job to do. If we all get too carried away with feelings and what the group thinks, we get bogged down in too much nothing. It's exciting to be free, even if it is just like a butterfly," and she fluttered her way out the door, sort of.

CHAPTER 8.
LUNCH

KAYLEEN MERINGUE WAS ALMOST ALWAYS
the first student out when the lunch bell rang. She loved that
sense of freedom when she could leap through the double
doors out into the world of fresh air—and the School Canteen. The whole process revitalised her, and helped her to cope
with the inevitability of two more lessons when the eating part
was done. Trudging behind came her best pal Sheila Nutter,
although nobody could realistically work out why these two
were friends. One so full of energies waiting to be explored,
while the other was as sour as a Space Pickle!

Kayleen also loved lunch, while Sheila hardly ever ate anything. Every day, Kayleen leaped with joy towards the School
Canteen, with a little pink purse in hand, ready to explore the
day's delicacies. Sheila usually had one Salada Cracker already
snapped in two, and filled with the meanest and leanest scraping
of Vegemite. She trudged behind Kayleen to the School Canteen
anyway. Well, she had nowhere else to go.

"Hang on, Sheila, just getting a few bits and pieces. It's
Wednesday, Sheils, my favourite Canteen day."

Sheila gave her twangy, moany voice a bit of an airing, "Kayleen,
every day they've got the same food! Come on, or the Form 2
drop-kicks will get our spot. I'll give you a bite of my Salada."

"Sheila, I'd rather stick pins in my eyes." Just the thought of
that offer made Kayleen sick to the stomach. No way! She had

purchases to make and she was going to make them, big time, so she dived into the queue of thousands who had arrived, and managed to come up for air right at the front.

"Yes, Kayleen, the usual today?" asked Mrs DiCarlo, the Canteen boss with the strangely floppy arms.

"Yes please, Mrs D, but today I'll have two of everything. So that'll be two salad sandwiches, pasties, tomato soups in a cup, iced donuts, jam donuts, Jam Fancies, Chocolate Royals, Wagon Wheels, chocolate coated wholemeal biscuits; oh, and peanut butter sandwiches. One more thing, a Block in Bread. Well, that's what my dad likes to call it."

"Are you sure that'll be enough?" smiled Mrs DiCarlo, but she didn't push the issue because she knew Kayleen lived with her dad and five brothers after her mum had left a couple of years ago for reasons unspoken about. But why the double load today?

"Well, aren't you the lucky lady today, Kayleen. Today we've got a special on. A free purchase of whatever the winner likes. And by winner we mean … hang onto your brain … we mean …the first person to come up to the Canteen whose name starts with … K! Well, what do you know? K, that's you Kayleen, go and enjoy your feast, and congratulations."

Sheila was unmoved. "You know they'll make you pay for it down the track. Like me Mum says, 'Ya don't get nothin' for nothing."

"Ah Sheila, sometimes people just like to do nice things."

"Yeah right, maybe."

Well, luckily some of the group had managed to claim their favourite spot while Kayleen ordered her provisions, so they joined them on the concrete path: Con, Umame, William and Bobby. I was just standing a little to the side, officially observing, but basically not knowing what to do.

"Where's your lunch, Ek," said William, and this was probably the most he'd ever said at the school, according to later reports.

"Oh, don't worry, William. I didn't really know what to do, this being my first day here. In Dutch, we always go home for lunch. It doesn't matter. I'm still full from all the excitement."

"Bull dust! No eat, no brains! That's what my Yiayia always says," offered Con.

"I can give you some money so you can get something from the Canteen."

"You're all too late!" shouted Kayleen, who was severely weighed down by her bags of goodies, reminding me of a certain relative I recently shared an Oktokraft with. "Here you go, Ek, a fully equipped quality A-1 lunch for you on your first day in this little, nice and not-so-nice school. Just enjoy it Ek, and we'll just say it's a share lunch from all of us."

I looked quickly at Sheila, and I really thought she was going to be sick, but I had learned enough today to realise that the dark forces might have hidden engines that we can't always see.

I realised something about these students. Whatever situation came up, they responded like a tapestry, knowing how to blend the care and laughter threads to create a positive whole. I faced them, so grateful.

"Thanks everyone, very much. Wow, that's so nice of you. Food. Heaps of food! I might just leave this block in bread till later though. A snack after school, maybe. Thanks, thanks!"

Umame burst in to speak. "OK guys, move in close so nobody can listen in. This morning before I came to class, I ran into my sister, Oksana in Form 2. Well, she said there's a whole lot of stuff happening, and there could be a few explosions this afternoon."

"Like what explosions, Umame? You're such a drama queen!" Bobby didn't like problems or conflict. It seemed that his popular defence was laughter, and it had got him a long way so far.

"Guys listen. I don't know too much yet, other than this is big! Oksana said we need to be ready. Let's meet behind the Canteen after school. In the meantime, think about what your most successful but annoying qualities are to get in people's faces. We know yours, Sheila!" Quick as a flash she ran off to get herself a much needed Wagon Wheel. Sheila stared after her, clearly thinking that, in some circumstances, a prison sentence wouldn't be so bad. Then she secretly smiled to herself. Umame was gold.

"Hey Sheila, are you related to Mr Glass?"

Anyone could have made this crack, and this time Sheila didn't have a whip-cracking answer. She just had to stand there and listen to the chorus of ridicule. Kayleen stood there too, looking very worried and alone.

I could certainly sense, with or without artificial help from the Panel, that Bobby Gee couldn't stand it if things got a bit rough. Umame understood this. She explained, largely for my benefit, that she and Bobby had known each other since they were in Prep, and they had often gone to each other's houses to play or just sit and talk. The two were quite a team in the friendship stakes, and I thought about how lucky they were.

Umame explained further. "Bobby's parents own the local Chinese Restaurant in Springvale called The Chow Palace. His great-great-grandfather had been in Australia since the Gold Rush days. He started off, like many, in the Ballarat fields, which were so crowded with prospectors from all over the world that, frankly, nobody expected too much, even though they still tried to cling desperately to hope."

Bobby was refuelled with confidence thanks to Umame, and he continued by himself. "Then, one day, Grandpa struck it lucky in the Gold Rush. He discovered a three-ton nugget worth all of Melbourne, and more. But, of course, as fate would have it, he lost the lot in a poker game. He had nothing, went into a bit of a dark time, and so my grandmother went out to work. She joined the Touring Company of The Great Peking Circus, and she taught me this little trick, which I will show you now."

A chorus of "Wow" and "You ripper" and "Bobby for Prime Minister" went around the group, as they fixed their eyes on

Bobby in great anticipation.

When the expectant audience were finally still, Bobby kicked his left leg up above his head, while still standing on his right foot. He gripped his left ankle with both hands and started hopping frantically.

"Hey Kayleen," he squeaked from his uncomfortable position, "lie down!"

"What for? No way!"

"Go on! I'll jump over you!"

"Don't be a tool, Bobby. What if you land on me?"

"Won't, Kayleen. Honest. I've never fallen on anybody before! It's called a Chinese Lunge Jump!"

Lost for some reasonable reply, Kayleen heaved her food-filled frame on the ground, and she lay on her back.

With great precision, Bobby manoeuvred himself beside Kayleen, still gripping his leg with a distinct look of uncertainty.

"OK everyone, countdown from twenty and I'll jump across my beautiful assistant."

"Noooo," screamed Kayleen. "Countdown from three sounds heaps better. Sheila, go ring Tobin Brothers!"

"Three … two … one … jump!" And with one almighty leap, Bobby, still clinging to that leg above his head, flung himself across Kayleen, who had her eyes shut so tight they wouldn't open. The crowd cheered Bobby as though he was the circus star himself, bowing deeply and thanking his supporters. "Phew, that was lucky!"

"What do you mean, lucky?" asked Kayleen, suddenly very wide-eyed.

"Because in the Great Peking Circus my Grandmother was an usherette!"

Massive laughter followed, and Bobby knew he'd done it again; he hadn't lost his touch. Even on a day like this.

Kayleen got up as though she'd been through an Interstellar Konflict. "Arms and legs, eh Ek?" she suddenly said to me. "Who on earth would have thought it would all get as confusing as this? I don't worry about anything, and you shouldn't either."

It was as if she could read my mind.

I must admit that I had experienced quite a spectacular morning so far in this funny little place. So much seemed to float around the minds of these Blue-Green Planet dwellers, and I, at each turn of events, felt just that bit stronger inside myself. Maybe I was happy that I'd been sent on this mission, although I was of course very aware that I'd done nothing in that regard. Then again, I'd only been here for one morning, so plenty of time yet!

Then again, I wasn't ready for a visit from Oksana. She looked just like Umame and had the same driven, urgent way of speaking.

"Listen guys, just here to tell you. Around the back of the school, some heavies are giving a lot of kids a hard time, screaming at them, trying to hurt them, you name it."

"What? You mean the Form 4 heavies?"

"No, it's the teacher heavies. They're all trying to catch kids and tie them to the pylon. Their eyes are wild and spiralling around in their heads. Maniacs. Just be really careful." And then she ran off, goodness knows where.

Everyone stood frozen, not sure of what to do. Most surprisingly, I had an idea. Back home it was a bit of a game, but I saw no reason why it couldn't work just as well with a different purpose.

"OK everyone, listen here. I've seen this done. Everyone, clasp someone's arm like a Roman handshake, whatever that is, so we're in a chain nice and tight. We'll run round the back and if we spot any adults behaving badly, and I can tell you I've seen a few in my life, we just shut our eyes and run at breakneck speed in their direction. I tell you it's a win-win. They're so shocked when they see us coming they just stop their nonsense. Then wham, we just run them over. They might be a little stunned, but not really hurt."

They stood and stared at me.

"Wow," said Bobby, "this 'Dutch' place must be pretty amazing. Let's do it! Cool, Ek."

Unfortunately, our arm clinching preparations were suddenly

interrupted by a snivelling, high-pitched voice on the Intercom.

"Save that thought, Ek, we can do this later. It's too good to rush."

"This is Miss Dullard speaking, the particular favourite of the Ministry of Education. You will soon hear a bell ring." Straight away the school bell sounded shrill across the grounds. She continued, "There we go. What a beautiful sound! You are all required at Assembly at once. Girls, please wear your hats and blazers. Boys must wear ties and blazers. No slobs. After the Assembly, we will go straight to Period 6 before home."

The Form 1 group had no idea who she was. Luckily, Mrs DiCarlo walked past with arm-loads of unbought goodies. "Don't worry, she's just the crochet teacher, tries really hard to make friends with Mr Glass," she explained while handing out dozens of Arnott's Jam Fancies, "don't stress."

CHAPTER 9.
ASSEMBLY

WE AMBLED ACROSS TO THE quadrangle after grabbing extra uniform bits along the way. I must say, I was struck by the hat and tie business. The girls' hats looked distinctly like Mooncakes plonked on their heads, while the boys' ties were totally like floppy versions of an Oktopus arm. I could only laugh very quietly, of course.

The quadrangle had been so arranged that all teachers could sit in comfortable armchairs, while all students had to stand the whole time. This seemed unusual, but who am I to make a comment. There was Mr Glass and his pal Mr Stipple the P.E. Meister, and his pal Miss Susie Dullard, the crochet teacher. Then came the beloved Mr Gently, Mrs (Ini and Itu) Lorelei, and Mr Jurgen Bleach, a new and young Maths teacher who we were to have Period 6. Oh, and at the front was a piano, the proud world of Mrs Rita Von Beethoven the music teacher, and her favourite student Margaret—who didn't have to wear a hat in case it fell on the keyboard mid-tune.

Miss Dullard, and there were some who noticed her entire outfit had been crocheted in Asteroid-green fibre, including her shoes, rose to address the crowd. A few of us looked over at the Headmaster, and quite frankly, Mr Glass looked old and frail, slumped in his armchair, as though the entire day so far had been too much. His eyes were distant and glazed, and he didn't seem to me like the man I'd come across this morning. I had seen some clearly different behaviour from him earlier, but had other things happened in his world today that I didn't know about? Miss Dullard began to speak.

"Before we start on the most important business of the day, and you all know what that is, there are two matters Mr Glass has asked me to go through first.

Point one: twelve girls do not have a hat. Girls, hats are our identity as ladies and mothers of babies to come. No hats indicates a desire for a nation that is dried up and childless. How dare you! Come forward now and I'll give you some alternative hats to help you remember this. Mrs Lorelei, please."

Awkwardly as usual, Mrs Lorelei pulled this grey mass from under her armchair: metal classroom bins. She had to hand one to each hatless girl to wear instead. At the end of this nasty ceremony, the girls slumped back embarrassed, and Mrs Lorelei flopped into her armchair, ashamed. It was as though the fibre of normality had dropped out of this community, but how was I to know? I was the new boy. All the same, what if I was somehow responsible?

"Point two, boys and girls: as personal confidant of Mr Glass, I must say that we've noticed that the main school troublemakers—of which there are many, have foreign names. As in, not English names from the Motherland, like Mudd, Blood and Gherkinsquasher."

She continued her rant. "Evidence always precedes a conclusion, so it's clear that some of you don't speak very much English. It's time to learn, by observing. Anyone who does not have a

British name must move right to the back, and you real Anglos, dash to the front, please." And this last bit was uttered with the broad smile of common ancestry.

I could feel huge waves of anger and resentment from my Form 1 classmates. I wasn't surprised, for this sort of action would never have occurred in Learning Pods at home. How would these students handle all this?

"That's you and me, mate," said Con. "Foreigners. This is what makes me really sick. They take one look at a kid's face or name, and the judgement's made; back of the line. Like we've got nothing to offer anyway, because we're different. Now we're not allowed to be different any more. Ignorance has spoken."

"Not loud enough, Con," I replied, "leave her to me."

Con looked surprised, but a little bit proud too. 'A new warrior in the Form 1 Battalion,' he probably thought. He did not realise this was way bigger than Westall High School, and that I was a member of the ULTERIATA BLACK HOLE GALAXY SUPERMASSIVATA Royal Family. And nobody pushes us around, or our citizens. Right at this point, though, I felt I had some new citizens of my own to care for.

All us 'failed citizens' walked slowly to the back. I saw even Bobby was pushed towards us, whose family had been Australians since the Gold Rush.

"Well done, all of you. Right, now stand and sing the school song."

The voice had changed. The sound was shrill, self-seeking and cruel. Miss Dullard spun around and, in her descent to the armchair cushion, I couldn't help notice Mr Stipple's hand slide across to pat a crocheted bottom. I don't think it was entirely intentional when she sat on it.

Mrs Rita Von Beethoven bounded to the front. For years she had been a leading soprano with the Williamstown West Operatic Group, but this advanced work in no way lessened her love for music and young people. She had been at Westall High School since its inception just a few year earlier, and she could only remember good times. She signalled to her favourite student, Margaret Glass, who was at the keyboard, and they were off.

Noble Westall soil of Britain

Strike thy chords with tones so bright

Let our gracious Queen be smitten

By our Nation's beaming light

Power of Scotland's purple heather

All that's great we clearly see

Swans of Wales wear God's white feather

Where in Westall we might be.

Well, that is to say, Margaret and Mrs Von Beethoven might have been off and running, but the students' lips were eerily tight and produced very little. The more Margaret pounded the keys, the less they sang. The more Mrs Von Beethoven chirped her outrageous ornamentations and trills, the more the students actively stopped breathing, so no note would escape from their mouths. The whole thing ground to a pathetic finish, with even Margaret throwing in the odd fist where delicate fingers might have been intended. I could see the glimmer of a tear in Mrs Von Beethoven's left eye. I didn't feel too great myself.

Susie Dullard resumed what she had taken to be her rightful place at the front of the assembly.

"Thank you, Mrs Von Beethoven, I'm sure that has eclipsed even your previous high standards." Was this woman profoundly deaf? "So now, let's all stand for The Creed, shall we? Come on, up!" She seemed to have forgotten that all students were already standing. And so it began.

> I love God and my country,
>
> I'll honour the flag
>
> I'll serve the Queen
>
> And cheerfully obey my parents, teachers and the laws.

And it was at this point that I snapped into a hundred pieces. I felt my face morph into tomato red, and I stalked to the front of the teacher crowd. Behind me I could hear Con urging me not to say anything stupid, but at the same time he and the others managed a genuine, "Good on ya, Ek!"

I started, and in a way I could already pity my little audience.

"Now you listen to me! I haven't been here very long. No one has bothered to welcome me formally into this ridiculous place. I have arrived in what seems like a civil war. I speak English perfectly well, and I've been shoved to the back with a group of students who also speak English perfectly well. There is this belief that young people are bad right from the inside, and it's the ridiculous selfishness of some of you lot that is supposed to save us. Well let me tell you this! I will not participate in this Creed! It's too much, way, way too much! I come from a fine nation called … Dutch. In Dutch, we have a wise, kind, yet powerful King, and he is married to our Queen. Without recourse to bleating little sentences, of course we honour and follow and love them, but they do the same for us. So I will never, ever betray this by offering all my loyalties to a queen I have never even heard of. Never. It's totally rude to even ask this, let alone assume and expect. I will not do it just because I am a child."

Silence. Absolute extreme, total, forbidding silence. No child had ever spoken like this before, and in such a passionate manner. Did children even have feelings?

Mr Glass, the Headmaster, rose from his seat. He still looked like he'd been dragged through a Kosmic Storm without a safety helmet. Something had happened.

With great force, I surrounded Mr Glass, but no one else, with a powerful beam, called The Intergalactic Magnetic Relocation, which pushes out a type of energy to isolate a Being in need from a troublesome event and gives him some renewed strength.

"Ek, listen. You don't have to participate if you don't want to.

Just sit out when the others say it."

"What's happened to you, Mr Glass? You were such an unpleasant and scary man this morning."

"I know. Ek, listen. Dullard and Stipple aren't real teachers. They work for the Ministry of Education. Their task is to remove all rights and powers from children. It's a national movement called 'The Revised Mind'. They believe serious learning will take over children's minds, so this group will do anything to disturb their development: separatism, no effort, total obedience, meaningless values, stupid songs; you name it. Engineering this wasn't too bad at the start, but then two of the Ministry operatives arrived because I wasn't moving the program fast enough. I wasn't dragooning our children into sameness fast enough. I thought I could get away with being Mr Angry all over the place, but my heart was just not in it, regardless of what most of the students thought. But worse, Ek, I have two children of my own, and I've just learned that they've been kidnapped. Those two did it. I'm trapped. Please help me!" He started crying, very softly.

I had to help. This wasn't about 'young me' Ek. This was about Prince Ek, who could bring about change!

I started by revealing my identity to Mr Glass, the first time I had done so on this odd, Blue-Green Planet. Mr Glass saw a divine shimmering of immense beauty, on a familiar looking figure, an Oktopus.

"You have tentacles," said Mr Glass in wonderment.

"They're Arms, actually, but listen. After this so-called assembly, you must go home, and I will be in touch. All this vicious rubbish aimed at destroying children's lives has to stop. And it will. I'll revise a few minds of my own."

I faded back to my drab Westall self. I hoped I had done the right thing. Doesn't everybody, most of the time?

Dullard the Drab, as she had become in my mind, rose to speak again. 'A Ministry agent,' I thought to myself. What black-hearted organisation would keep children from asking questions and forming conclusions? Then she spoke again.

"Mr Glass, you may have noticed that, when I spoke before, not everyone paid attention to me. Would you like to address this please?"

I could see Mr Glass struggle, as he quietly said, "No, no I wouldn't", and he dragged himself away from the group, a broken man, but hopefully digesting the crumb of hope that I had just thrown to him.

"Well, I certainly would," burst in Mr Stipple, "and I've got a lot to say. Fix your eyes on me! Fix your eyes on me! Anyone from the weediest string bean to the greatest fatso among you who even dares to fix their eyes anywhere but on me, could very well have them pulled out with the vacuum cleaner. But not before their arms and legs are amputated, of course. I'm just going to ask you a teeny question: what happened here today at our beloved Westall High School? What did you see? You can trust me. Just tell me, OK?"

There was silence for a bit, but then William, our very much loved William, said with some courage, "We all watched a spaceship land in The Grange."

A severe silence followed. Mr Stipple turned a shade of vile purply-orange, and his eyes seemed to fight against a natural desire to explode. His mouth became two little black strings highlighting white blotches that came and went among the purple mix.

"What?" he screeched in his nastiest voice. "You! You boy! You with the unwashed hair! Get up here so I can make sure you will never forget this day, or you will never be able to remember it!"

With great, sadistic gusto, Stipple lurched towards William, then dragged him, first by the arms then by his feet along the rows of all the students, up the stairs and along the reclining teachers, into the building and an unknown space not too far beyond. Sounds were audible from within, of disciplinary weapons colliding with William's young and frail body, and of the suffering boy himself. William groaned and cried out, clearly in so much pain that he could stand no more. After what seemed an eternity of blow upon blow, Mr Stipple reappeared, rubbing his hands.

"Well now, we all know what that stupid boy said wrong, don't we?"

"Yes Mr Stipple," came a whispering chorus.

A hush. "And what did you all see?"

Silence. A stronger attempt.

"Well?"

Silence. Even more so. Digging in.

"Weeeell?"

Silence. With force. No one was prepared to betray William in this way.

"I'll tell you what you all saw," and he waited a bit, just long enough for us all to hear William from inside, crying desperately from the pain, "you saw nothing! Nothing at all. Nothing!"

This manic outburst proved to me the truth of Mr Glass' claims about a Stipple-Dullard takeover of the school, under the authority of the Education Ministry. How stupid was it all, that these kids were being forced to say they had seen nothing, when I was part of the very thing they weren't supposed to have seen. What ridiculous beings lived here? I chose to stay quiet for now, but a stirring inside me told me there was more trouble at hand. I noticed Mr Stipple staring at Mr Gently.

"Well, well, well," said Mr Stipple heading for that purple effect again, "here he is, Mr Good Old Gently, the leader of the pack. Hey kids, I can see things with my big camera, but oh diddums I've lost my little camera, why don't you follow me, I'm the Pied Piper, just step into my cave of stupidity." All that outraged ridicule was spat out at typewriter rate, and most of it straight into Mr Gently's face.

Mr Gently just stood there. Calm, serene, somehow very powerful. "One day the truth will come out, Mr Stipple."

"Oh, the truth, it's the truth you want, Mr Gently, the truth about you just wanting to do very little other than whatever you choose to do. Where's Mr Gently today? Goodness knows! Probably Luna Park with a bunch of students who haven't even signed themselves out! Where's Mr Gently right now? Who knows? Who ever knows? Who cares?"

Mr Gently spoke quietly and with great control. "You know none of that's true, Mr Stipple. I love my work here, and each day I see all my students grow with wisdom and learning."

Bobby giggled quietly. "I must've been away that day." Before he got a chance to come up with something else stupid, he was quickly gagged by Kayleen and a few others.

"You're a fool, Mr Gently, if you think we're all just going to buy this Superteacher lie. You saw nothing. You heard nothing, and if you'd like to continue working here, I suggest you don't say anything different. Got it? There are many ways that little show-off teachers can be destroyed, you know."

"No professional would ever speak like this in front of children, Mr Stipple. Don't threaten me. I know I have nothing to worry about, and neither do all these young people. You can make them chant, 'We Saw Nothing' like they're robotic morons, but not me. And one day, they'll feel deeply ashamed at what you've made them do. And by the way, do you think you could bring poor William out now, to be with us? I suggest strongly that you do that."

At this outrageous dare, and that was clearly how he saw this moment, Mr Stipple screamed for the police to come. By now, the tone of his voice rivalled the shrillness of a pop starlet. He suddenly lurched forward, distinctly foaming at the mouth, and fell promptly on the ground. Miss Dullard immediately began to employ some cardiac pounding to get him back to action, while Mrs Von Beethoven, the music maestro, happily obstructed her as she headed for the upright to lead the devoted community through The National Anthem. Young Margaret frantically turned the pages, although it was not at all odd that nobody sang along, the way they would have in my Black Hole Home.

I thought it was even odder that William seemed to have disappeared.

Con leaned over to whisper something to me. "Look, Mr Bleach has gone. He was sitting right up there with the others, and now he's gone. Right in the middle of World War 3. What's going on, Ek?"

"No idea, Con. Don't panic. Everything will be sorted soon, I just know it."

But the truth was, I didn't have a clue.

CHAPTER 10.
PERIOD SIX

THE MIND-SHATTERING ASSEMBLY HAD GONE over the planned time, not surprisingly, but our class had raced back to the classroom to make sure Mr Bleach was there. But he wasn't, so we all entered wondering where to go from here.

I stopped Umame at the door. "Quickly, go and find your sister Oksana and find out what the Form 2 kids are doing after school. We need them to be the most annoying and disruptive force this side of the Galactic Equator. It'll help them, as well as us!"

"OK, no worries. And thanks. There's something weird about you, Ek. One minute it's like you're totally lost and know nothing, and the next minute you're about a hundred years old, and powerful even. Just as well I like weird, isn't it? I won't be long. I need to know Mr Bleach is OK."

"Great, and tell them to go into action straight after school. I'm not going to tell them exactly what to do. The best person to solve a problem is yourself. Just tell them we little Form 1 kiddies expect, no, dare them to be brilliant at it. Then they will be."

Umame dashed off to rally the senior troops, while I went back inside the classroom.

"Who is this Stipple dead-head anyway?" asked Kayleen. "I don't remember him being here last year."

"He's a disgusting pig," answered Sheila. "He can't just talk to people like that. Not to Mr Gently, never. Mr Gently drove me and my mum to Prince Henry's when my dad was having his op. Mr Gently's all right, he's the best, so they'd better bloody lay off him."

"And then your dad … " said Kayleen, who at once changed her mind. Sheila looked down at her hands, and I thought she might cry. She didn't. She'd learned to be made of stronger stuff. It's hard when people have to be made of stronger stuff.

Pymble walked forward. This boy was usually a pretty quiet number, but now he was red in the face after all the to-do with the Stipple and Dullard show. "Hey, I've got an idea. It's a game I just made up, called 'Judge'. I'll think of a name, then all of you get to decide what to do with that person." Pymble spoke mainly to Sheila, as if to help her up get through this difficult moment. "And the first one is, um, Mickey Mouse!"

"A lifetime of free tickets to the Clayton Pool!"

"A Family Plate of Lemon Chicken from my dad's restaurant."

"Fired from Disneyland!"

And on they went, shrieking with laughter at each other's wild suggestions as they did a few more names.

"Right," said Pymble, "one last one—Mr Stipple." There was a raucous clatter of sharp laughter which gradually eased, then fell into a long, ghostly silence. Very quietly Pymble said, "This is why we have to act today. Some people fall outside normal behaviour, so that in the end, we can't even act because our brains won't even go down to their level. They've made us go numb. They're selfish pigs! Don't worry, Sheila."

A tear rolled reluctantly down Sheila's cheek. She missed her dad.

It was Bobby's duty to lift the mood. "Hey, Stipple and Dullard? Dullard and Stipple. Stullard and Dipple! Did you see what I saw? His hand looked like a shrivelled sultana after she sat on it. About five hours she strangled his little fingers. If only my mum could have been here; she loves sewing. She could have crocheted his hand right onto the dress. A forever dress."

"More like a hand me down!" offered Margaret the muso.

And another couple of minutes passed by as the young friends amused and supported each other with almost fanatical laughter.

A knock on the window, and with great speed the students slid into their seats, feigning interest in some imaginary teacher at the front. Interestingly though, the person at the outside window was Mr Bleach, signalling frantically to any and all to open the window quickly. As soon as that was organised, he asked for a group of about four students to stay by the window while he went to get something. He opened the boot of his station wagon and carried out a most precious parcel wrapped in a blanket. He passed this package safely into the waiting arms of the students, and everyone could see it was the limp body of William, so hurt, so delicate, but still alive.

Mr Bleach swiftly followed the very sad William bundle in through the window. "I went looking for him. I found him in the corridor, and I told him I'd take him home. He didn't want to. He wants to be here with you."

The students were pretty much agog with this new Mr Bleach. Con had filled me in on what he was normally like. He was always Mr Perfect, demanding the completest silence every lesson before any work could be done—even a breath was considered offensive. Then there was always his preliminary lecture. "Your work needs to be measured and precise. Your thinking processes must be equal to those of a French clock. Your calculations must rival the finest international mathematicians. Your final product, I insist, must stink of perfection, and you must too."

And here he was, saving the life of a very sick boy by smuggling him away from some savage and deranged attackers. William was so hurt, so damaged. From where I was sitting, I could see huge purple bruises. There were painful welts over his eyes. His body shivered involuntarily at the slightest move he made. I felt his agony. We all did. We were now all the more determined to bring some justice to this community.

"Ek!" I heard William's feeble voice call me, "Ek, I don't understand it all, but I think for a time, I was unconscious." His breathing was like a desperate gasping for the slightest whisks of air, "I was unconscious and yet I saw you. I don't know how to say this, but maybe this means something to you. And there's one thing I need you to know. Be careful, Ek. Dullard and Stipple are very suspicious of you. They want to hurt you too. Be careful. Stop them as soon as you can."

"Thanks, William. I know what to do." Frankly, I didn't have a clue, but I knew I'd have to deal with this later. Once William's eyes were shut again, I performed the Healing Skan on him, an old Oktopus healing method. Of course it had to be the compact version as I did not want to attract attention. The compact scan only required use of the eyes. By zig-zagging them everywhere, but fast and over a sick individual, health would be restored layer by layer. This restorative process was marvellous, and recovery was guaranteed as painless and speedy.

I could swear Mr Bleach had been watching me, and he said, "Thank you Ek. Thank you very much." Then he swung around to the class and announced, "Now everyone, there's not a lot of time left in this lesson, all because I was so late. I'm not too much of a French clock today, I realise. So, let me think. Something quick. Something to think about before the bell. I know, please write out the nine times table." Like a flash, the students flipped themselves around to the front, whipped out their exercise books and found a clean page. "Now start with:

0 times 9 = 0

1 times 9

2

3

4

5

6

7

8

9

10 times 9 = __ "

The students leaped at this task. Too easy! Who didn't know their nine times table? Laughter was beginning to return to the group, and it seemed as though Mr Bleach had found a new identity.

Amid the mathematical noise, William woke up, looked around at his mates, and smiled the smile of gratitude and deep friendship. He looked a snippet better already.

Mr Bleach egged the happy mob on. "Come on, hurry up, we don't have an eternity to do this little task that's really meant for three year olds," he joked.

"Well I shouldn't be doing it then, sir," replied Bobby, "I'm only two and a half!"

"You sure are!" shouted everybody."

"OK finished!"

"Finished!"

And so they finished, some of their youthful spirit restored. Mr Bleach asked, without even time for a ninth of a breath.

"So, what's so special about this exercise? Well, look at the columns going up, and those going down." Like a tornado had struck their minds, a chorus of "Wow!" And many other such words of instant approval rang around the classroom. The students also felt they were lucky to be in the presence of someone so gifted and special as Mr Bleach. He spoke again.

"Now then, the excitement continues. I would like you to do the same thing, but with the ninety-nine times table."

At that exact moment, the final bell rang.

"We'll do it for homework, sir," they all promised, and they seriously meant it.

"You've been terrific today, kids. I thank you. Oh, and don't forget your meeting behind the canteen. Good luck."

I looked at him. How did he know? How did so many things get known around here? Who was the mouth? In the meantime Mr Bleach had wandered over to William to take him home again, but when he approached William, he could not see a single bruise or wound left on him. Mr Bleach turned around to look at me.

I turned around and ran.

CHAPTER 11.
BEHIND THE CANTEEN

IT'S PROBABLY NOT EVEN WORTH my while saying that absolutely everyone was ready and eager behind the Canteen as instructed. It was quite a little force, now waiting in anticipation for their leader to speak. While I was there along with them, I suddenly remembered that I was their leader and, for once, I knew exactly what I wanted to say, and why I wanted to say it.

"Hi everyone, and thanks for coming to this meeting. You're probably thinking it's a bit odd that the new boy has called you all together, and it probably is. I guess all things are for a reason. We do things sometimes because they matter. But more about that later. First, we need to make sure we are safe. It struck me today that whatever new thing we talked about, there was always somebody who knew all about it already, as though there was some sort of underground network picking up on everything that was being said or done. This sort of thing doesn't happen by chance, so I thought to myself, who in this school gets to hear everything and talk to everyone? Well, it's obvious, but then it's wrong! Mrs DiCarlo, our Canteen lady. But come to think of it, she's the very picture of what is caring and good in this place. She gives freebies, and helps everyone, and has her kids at this school, and is the kindest person ever. So I thought, if it's not the Canteen lady, then—"

"It's something in the Canteen itself!" Con shouted. "Wait here, I'll have a squizz." He dashed eagerly around the corner to check out the mysteries of the Canteen. It didn't take him long to return, laden with tiny microphones, plugs and wires, inputs, earphones and more. "There's way more, Ek. Somebody's been using the Canteen as an Espionage Unit, only he's been a bit of a dumbo. Look here on this tag; it says T. Stipple, Ministry Agent."

A cry of outrage went through the crowd. To think they had accepted this jerk into their community. But that's what kids do, I suppose, they accept the new before they condemn.

"Great work, Bobby," I said, "and we'll deal with Stipple and his crocheted woman later, believe me. OK, we know Bobby's here of course, but let's see who else. I tell you now, with what we're about to do, every one of you will have a major part to play. First, there's the Form 2 Team of Coles and Ray. Guys, what did you do this afternoon?"

"We slipped out of the school to get to a phone box," said Coles, a very tall boy who got the nickname 'Coles' because the shop gave him a Saturday job when he was only nine years old. That's how tall he was, even then. Coles continued, "We rang the Clayton, Springvale, Noble Park and Heatherton Police Stations, just to reinforce the importance of our mission. We also gave the Army, Air Force and Navy a bell. We told them all some shocking crime had been committed against a child who had been severely brutalised in public."

"By Stipple and Dull," piped up Ray, a bit miffed that he hadn't had a chance to speak, "but we've got something pretty amazing lined up for these two."

"Dullard," said Coles.

"That's what I said, meathead," snapped Ray.

"You said 'Dull!"

"Well, she is!" And they went off laughing, happy as Larry.

I thanked the two ready-to-roll Form 2 boys for their after-noon's work. The crowd of fellow partisans cheered and clapped wildly. Next, I asked Scout to talk about her role. There was something sharp and alert about Scout, and when she spoke, the hypnotic energies she gave off were compelling; I felt sure she'd have something powerful to add.

"What upset me the most is that we are not allowed to say a word about what we all saw, and so many others as well. What's that supposed to mean? That kids are insignificant, untrust-worthy, they don't really count, or what? You tell me and I'll tell you you're wrong. So I asked myself, who can I get onto to help spread some important news of things that have been happening, say like today. The answer came to me like the light in Bambi's eyes. The press. So I've got a batch of them coming later: a huge mob of newspaper reporters, including one from 'The Truth', magazine writers, radio people, tv stations 2, 7, 9 and Channel O. Between them, everyone will be interviewed: eye witnesses, air flight experts, weather experts, balloon makers, professors of everything flight, landing and alien. Such a crowd will gather here that we will make world news. And nobody wants news about somebody who didn't see things. At the same time, this press gathering will be a perfect foil for what Coles and Ray are doing at the back of the school. It's a win-win!"

There was another spontaneous outbreak of noisy support. I had one niggling concern though; I didn't know what a 'Bambi' was! I thought maybe this was not the best time to bring this up.

"Scout, brilliant stuff, I tell you what! Now, one more Form 2 speaker. Berenice?"

"Thanks Ek, and my story's a bit different. This morning, when the strange craft was slowing down above the school, I said to my best friend Maya that we should run after it a bit and see what it did. Well, it was heading for The Grange. Maya's a better runner than me so she got there faster. By the time I turned the corner, the saucer thing was landing, and Maya was right next to it. Then, all of a sudden, she screamed this hysterical scream and then fainted. I shouted to some kids behind me to get some help, as in medical help. I was on the ground next to Maya. As I reached out to hold her hand, the machine took off again, straight up vertical, then away like instantly, and it was gone. I stayed waiting for the ambulance. Maya whispered something to me, but it was so soft and weak it made no sense. She whispered, 'I saw half-boy half-dunno drop something.' A couple of minutes later an ambulance came. The officer said I wasn't to worry, Maya'd had a bit of a shock and she'd be home again tonight. So that's what I'd like to do later, visit her at home."

"Berenice, I think we'd all like to come with you. Poor girl," I said. "Thank you, Form 2, very much. This whole operation will, I'm sure, be most successful with so many brilliant young minds working all together."

While everyone clapped so responsively it seemed that the whole Canteen might collapse, I did feel some severe regret that Maya's vision of terror had in fact been me, and the dropped item was my Panel. It had never been my slightest thought to drag some innocent person into this totally unrelated mission of an alien boy lost in a field of young human beings. Come on Ek, don't cave in at this. Keep it moving. You're in control! Slowly, I moved again.

"There is much more to be done that I will reveal when we're off the school property. For now, though, I'd like to say this. As you probably all know by now, I'm Dutch, and this is my first day at Westall High School. You can imagine, I'm sure, my horror and disgust at what this first day has been like, and why I got so angry at that stupid assembly. I know there's a different way for children. Things are very different in Dutch. Children have an opportunity to talk about things that matter to them, to be safe and wise and creative and have fun in a world where all age groups take care of each other. I don't think this is a school where such fairness exists. Do I think it could exist? Yes, I do, and it has to be up to us tonight to make it happen."

There was a grave silence, the silence of respect, the sort of silence my father, King Ok, used to hear after he had spoken.

"Does anyone have any questions?"

Kayleen shot her hand up.

"Um, Ek, when you were in Dutch, did you live in a windmill?"

The whole group burst out in fits of laughter and groans of, "Oh, Kayleen!" No matter how much she was rubbished in fun, she stuck to her guns.

"Great question, Kayleen," I said, "and remind me to give you an answer tonight. OK, we've heard from Form 2. The Form 1 team will get their instructions later. Don't be shocked, but we've got a few teachers here too. Not all teachers are bad eggs. Thank you, Mr Bleach and also Mrs Von Beethoven, our beloved music teacher." More applause echoed for these two teachers who were human too. "And last but not least, our terrific teacher of Indonesian, Mrs Mavis Lorelei!"

And like one great, enormous voice, all the students shouted out together, "INI AND ITU!"

"Now, last of all, against all the odds, someone who suffered cruelties and hardships that no one should ever have to endure … I welcome back our brave friend, William!"

The attack on William had left such an effect on everyone, that they all stood near him, quietly, out of respect.

"Onya, William."

"And then there's one further person, not here now but he'd like to be, later, if you give him permission. It's the Headmaster, Mr Glass." I knew the fallout that would come from this. Someone who had been so rude and unpleasant, so unbending and permanently coiled up like a tense spring. Everyone saw him as a

117

hater of young people. "Again, I'm going to ask you to trust me in this. What I can tell you is that this afternoon he was told his own children had been kidnapped, but this was another vile lie to try and break this man. So now, as an apology, he would like to join us for what is ahead. What do you say?"

Con spoke, "It's a big ask, Ek, he can be such a difficult fellow. But then again, who tells someone their children have been kidnapped?"

Coles came forward and said, quite proudly, "Perhaps you'd like Ray and me to take care of this matter tonight, Ek." And Ray stepped forward, "And perhaps the Headmaster might like to consider a fresh, new position to get this horror out of his mind, while we consider a new Headmaster."

"Proceed, guys," I said to these fine operators, as I knew exactly what they meant. "OK, now this is how it's going to be for tonight. Form 2, you're brilliantly organised. Form 1, we need stuff: food supplies, medical kits, blankets, diving equipment, plastic tanks; be creative with your own thoughts and ideas. Go and rummage for whatever you can find. I'm sure Mrs DiCarlo won't mind if we pick up a few things from her Canteen. Go home and tell your parents you need to go out for a while. They'll be able to see by the expressions on your faces that you mean business. Great parents are like that."

I remembered how pathetic and snivelling I had been when I was told I had to set out on my own mission. Even though I could sense that I was active in encouraging these young people to take control over their lives, I felt inside myself that I would never overcome my mother's words. They were a dagger that stuck permanently in my brains and heart.

"Next," I started as I made myself push through this barrier of both hurt and self-pity, "Con, in the middle of all that electronic stuff from the Canteen, did I see a mobile field telephone set?"

"Sure Ek, good spotting. Here it is."

"Thanks. We're going to need an in the field Communications Director, who will be stationed here in Westall High School."

"Why does he keep saying Westall High School all the time? We just say Westall."

"Because he's Dutch, stupid," explained Kayleen.

"Now, I'd like the Communications Director to be Sheila Nutter."

It looked as though Sheila was going to be marvellously happy, overwhelmed and sick all at the same time.

"Sheila's forgotten how terrific she can be on the inside, but she's super smart. Sheila, you can choose your own assistant who will be at the other end."

"Thanks, thank you," she uttered while coping with a very red and hot face, "I choose Kayleen, if that's OK."

"That's fantastic, Sheila, and don't forget it's not up to me. Be your own woman, no matter what. Every bit of information must go through you."

Kayleen was more than happy with her move too, and Ek knew the two were very effective together.

"And Umame and Con, could you be in charge of everything else we might come across along the way?"

"Sure could," confirmed Umame.

"Dare to be different!" shouted Con, rather like this catchcry had been burning a hole in his throat for some time.

They both nodded happily, but there was one more huge hurdle to cross.

"Bobby, a mountainous job for you, absolutely enormous!" Bobby swelled with pride and self-importance. What could this specialised task be?

"Bobby, could you please ring your dad in the restaurant to tell him there'll be about twenty of us coming for dinner."

Of course, Bobby the clown had just been clowned out. Everyone burst out laughing at him, but he was already on his Malvern Star and he shouted, "I'll just ride around and tell him. Make sure he cooks the good stuff. Maybe just a dry cracker for you, Ek!" and he was off.

"OK guys, go home and get whatever you need, and we'll meet at the Chow Palace at 6 Okts, I mean o'clock. And teachers, please bring your cars—with trailers."

CHAPTER 12.
CHOW PALACE

OF COURSE, AT PRECISELY 6 OKTS everyone was either gathered outside, or within eyeshot of the Chow Palace. Mr Bleach was the very first to arrive, and he'd let me know that wonderful Mr Gently wanted to come too, but he'd join us later. He didn't want his issues to become the important ones.

As everyone rolled up, someone asked me where they should put their goods that they'd found to take with them. All I said was, "You'd better ask Umame and Con. They're the boss." And of course Umame and Con were already at work just around the corner, stacking, packing, sorting and doing whatever it takes to run an efficient exodus. If only I'd had their help on board the Oktokraft with all of Mother's luggage.

All present, everything safely stowed away for later, we all entered.

When you've just come from a Black Hole, there could be nothing more striking and contrasting than the Chow Palace in Springvale. The minute I stepped across the threshold, I realised my life was entering a whole new phase. Inside this 'Palace', I had to agree that indeed it was, but in every way opposite to what I knew at home. Every smallest Okt of this space was decorated with the most powerful and dazzling designs and colours. The walls consisted of metallic red and gold shapes that looked like strong coded messages. The ceilings were blue with gold, but this time the gold designs looked like huge, sleek flying beings, for they had the most beautiful black eyes. On the floor there was a carpet of swirling green, with different textures depending on where you stood. Everywhere there were sparkling streamers of purple and silver, with large papery balls of pale orange suspended at every corner. I was so thrilled by this palatial vision that I asked Bobby what one of those gold, coded symbols meant.

"That one says Ice Cream," he said, "and that one says Rice, and the last one ... um ... egg fifty cents extra!"

How impressive is that, to wrap your most humble messages in gold! I felt so at home in this palace. It was so artistic and literate, and yet so useful when its basic purpose was to feed people.

There was one very large, round table all set up for us, with white cloths and intense red birds, one for each chair. We all found a seat, and I tried to pick up my red bird, but it just seemed to fall apart as it unrolled before my eyes and became just a piece of material. "Don't drop your serviette, Ek," Kayleen muttered. We all wondered what we would be eating tonight; this was an 'Earth First' experience for me, so I was particularly excited.

A lady suddenly appeared, looking like she'd been poured into a gold snakeskin. Umame leaned forward and said, "That's Bobby's Mum. During the day she's a teacher at Noble Park High, but then she sometimes comes and helps out at night."

"What does she teach?" I wondered.

"Double Bass. Her dad used to be in the Melbourne Symphony Orchestra."

"What's her name?" I asked.

"Auntie. Well, that's what everyone calls her."

Auntie moved into the centre of the room. "OK everybody, I've got a bowl here full of fortune cookies. They have never been wrong. And they taste great! Who'd like to go first?"

Like they had all read each other's minds, a loud chorus of "Mr Bleach! Mr Bleach!" rang around the restaurant.

"Looks like it's you, Mr Bleach. Here, take a fortune cookie, and let's hear your fortune."

Mr Bleach rummaged around the bowl for a while, picked up his fateful cookie, snapped it open and read, "Very soon, before the rice grain swells, you will meet not one, but two very beautiful women."

"Oooooooooooh!" went everybody.

"Sounds pretty good to me," said Mr Bleach laughingly, and as soon as he sat down, two huge kisses were planted on his cheeks, one from Mrs Von Beethoven, and one from Mavis Lorelei. Mr Bleach turned a distinct shade of red, poor thing.

"I told you they're never wrong," Auntie shouted above the laughter.

I leaned forward. "Hey Umame, if everyone calls her Auntie, then what does Bobby call her?"

"Mum," and she gave me a look that said, 'just where are you from, Ek?'

"One more," said Auntie. "How about that girl over there. You look a bit sad, love, are you worried about something?"

It was Berenice, and she nodded. Auntie smiled a very warm smile and offered her the bowl. Berenice took out a cookie and read, "Some things are solved, but we learn this later." It wasn't too clear what Berenice thought, but she did sit down in a calmer state, smiling ever so slightly.

"OK! Last one, and this is Auntie's choice, and I choose"—at this point she spun around with her bowl and let out such a high shrieking note that I thought she might choke. Everyone leaned forward as far as they could—"You!"

It was me, and this sort of public figure I hadn't imagined turning into.

"Ek Ek Ekekekekekekekekekekek," came the supporting chorus.

I let my fingers dangle into the bowl, and pulled out my fate. Snap, and read.

"We've caught a fraud, who's fought abroad.'

There it was, my whole story in a biscuit. Would they know, or just laugh it off? I hadn't even realised they were all laughing away. I looked around the room and it looked like they would have laughed at anything. Extreme hunger, I reckon. Fraud indeed! Where's the food? And there's Mr Bleach giving me the thumbs up now. What is it with that guy?

In came Bobby's dad, at last, juggling a mountain of dishes filled beyond the limit with the most mouth-watering delicacies.

"What are all these yummy-yummy things, Mr Gee?" asked Mrs Von Beethoven, "I don't know where to start first. This is such a treat. My husband never wants to go out anywhere to eat. Bacon and Toast, Crackers and a Cheese Slice. That's all he lives for. Oh, and his cup of Milo!"

Mr Gee replied, "Mrs Von Beethoven, I'm sure he is so over-whelmed by your exotic talents and beauty, that food is a very distant second best for him."

"Mr Gee, thank you so very much. What a very kind thing to say. Oof, I'm feeling quite warm tonight. Oh my goodness. Margaret, did you hear that?"

"Sure did, Mrs Von Beethoven. You don't even need a fortune cookie, the truth just came to you!"

"Anyway," said Mr Gee who probably hadn't intended his little joke to become so inflamed, "the dishes are, in order: Chicken Chop Suey, Lemon Chicken, Spring Rolls with Chicken, Chicken Chow Mein with Almonds, Chicken Chow Mein with Mushrooms, Chicken Chow Mein with Green Peppers, and Chicken Fried Rice."

"Boy, that's a lot of chicken," said Coles.

"Yeah," offered Kayleen, "Bobby's uncle has a chicken farm in Tootgarook!"

'Ah, Tootgarook, of course,' I thought to myself pointlessly.

Well, the dishes tasted as brilliant as they sounded, and everyone totally indulged themselves in this magnificent feast. After all they and I had been through, this was a fitting celebration of a milestone. A proper milestone, certainly, but there were more to come.

Given the amount of food that had been placed before us, I was amazed at how fast it was all consumed. Some of the kids even ate with those strange sticks that were lying all over the table, and which I thought were for producing tasteful applause. I guess I wasn't quite accustomed to the ways of this Blue-Green Planet just yet, nor its citizens who inhabited Westall High School, much as I liked them.

All platters, bowls and plates were swiftly cleared away, and the massive tablecloth was bundled up like a loaf of bread and taken away. From underneath the cloth there emerged a magnificent stage, glittering and polished, jewelled and sparkling. Auntie's double bass was swept up onto the stage, and Mr Gee jumped up carrying his keyboard. I heard Margaret gasping that it was one of those new ones that had chords as well as notes. I couldn't quite figure out why anyone would need a chord machine since, well, you know what I'm going to say. I've already told you so much about music back at home. Last to leap up was Bobby with a small rhythm device that he banged around a bit.

Bobby spoke, "Before we treat you to a bit of music, could you let me know, when I say your name, what you'd like for dessert? Starting with … let me see … Ek!"

I wasn't sure what to say. How would I know about desserts here. Then I remembered what Bobby had told me about the gold coded symbol on the wall. Feeling relieved and confident, I pointed to the first one, the one that meant Ice Cream. The whole group erupted into the loudest and most humiliating laughter I had ever heard, and it went on for a very long time.

"Got you back, Ek! That one says 'TOILETS'! Ha! No worries, we can get you that if you like." The laughter continued, and I realised they had all been in on the joke, even William. And you know what I felt? Annoyed that I'd let them trick me, and proud that I belonged somewhere with people who cared enough to have a bit of fun with me.

While the laughter was still at a maximum, Bobby turned his banging machine upside down and pressed a big red button that was on it. The kitchen doors flipped open, and several small carriages laden with desserts and extra longs spoons rolled by themselves into the room.

"Help yourselves, everyone, dessert—but not from the toilet!" Everyone quickly took their favourite choice, and nibbled and licked away while Bobby and his parents produced some wonderful music with cascading notes, beautiful contrasts and strengths, and the softest hints of barely audible sounds.

"OK, who'd like to join us. What about you Mrs Von Beethoven?"

"Oh well, OK then, but can Margaret come up and share the keyboard with you, Mr Gee?"

Like a flash, Margaret was up there ready to roll. Mrs Von Beethoven somehow rolled herself onto the stage, crawled up to full height quite puffed out, and said, "Here's a little song I wrote tonight, inspired by our wonderful host, Mr Gee. Just impro, OK guys? Hit it kids!"

The superb combo plus Margaret resumed their amazing sounds, and slowly, but with great beauty and sensitivity, Mrs Von Beethoven began her emotional song.

A maiden fell for Chicken Chow Mein

The finest lass that he'd ever seen

Her husband he liked bacon and cheese

She threw him away with strength and with ease

What a shame, he drowned in the Seven Seas.

You'd imagine it could be hard to pull off a standing ovation while holding a large bowl of dessert and a long spoon, but they managed. They more than managed; in fact, they completely overwhelmed the talented singer, musicians and themselves as well. Dizzied by her outstanding success, Mrs Von Beethoven tripped a bit over a spare spoon, and slid in a not too glamorous way onto Umame and Oksana. General support came from every direction and they propped her back in her chair.

I also had an idea for some music, but I wasn't sure how it

would work, so I was a little hesitant when I started.

"Back home in Dutch, we used to make instant music; our whole group would perform for just one of us, like a special treat. So maybe that person could be, um, Mr Bleach. Please lie on your back on the table, Mr Bleach. Don't worry, you're perfectly safe. Now then, while Mr Bleach is lying there hoping to fall asleep, here's what we'll do. First, combo musicians, start playing some slow and beautiful patterns of all different sounds. Then, when you feel you're on a roll, we'll all start humming, slowly changing from one of the combo notes to another, with no real tune, with no words. Everyone makes their own patterns."

This explanation seemed to mesmerise a few of us, and sometimes it's better to do rather than just talk about, so I told the combo to begin. The effect was startlingly beautiful, and I brought in all the singers next. Now while I say singers, I don't mean trained singers, of course, but every day around the house noise makers, such as every single one of the students and their teachers. And yet, their sound was now celestial, with silver beams of the purest notes touching against and through each other, as well as with the divine combo. The music became like a huge building made of sound, hugging Mr Bleach like a spectacular gift.

I let things go for some minutes, and the music grew more and more glorious. I was aware that no one really wanted to stop, ever. Eventually, I requested a gradual dimming of the sound, leading to complete silence.

"Well, Mr Bleach?"

Mr Bleach opened his eyes. "Amazing, the most magnificent sounds, like magnetism. Superb and brilliant. Deeper than Mathematics. Thanks, Ek."

"Great, but I don't know why you're lying around, Bleach. Everyone! This place needs to be tidied up. Dishes need to be washed, dessert plates go back to the kitchen, floor swept, clean tablecloth and red bird thingies, then thank Mr Gee, Auntie and our very own Bobby. After that, go straight outside to meet your teachers to pack your goods and equipment into their cars. Who's finished?"

A groan of "as if" filled the restaurant, but all the same they were very happy to be a part of this whole adventure.

"Thanks, Auntie!"

"Best food, Mr Gee!"

"All on the house, guys!"

"Hey Ek, has anyone shown you where the toilets are yet? Over here! Haha!"

Little did they all know that they would soon be going into a very different reality.

CHAPTER 13.
MAYA VERDI

ONCE OUTSIDE, WE COULD ALL see how brilliantly
equipped we were for our journey. It seemed as though my
classmates and the small band of teachers had thought of
every possibility: ropes, string, tapes, warm clothes, Band-Aids,
megaphones, snack food, meal type food, fuel stoves, drinking
water, insect repellant, torches, sleeping bags, blankets, Swiss
Army knives and, of course, kilos of PK Chewing Gum.

It took a bit of an effort to squeeze everyone into the three cars,
given how much amazing luggage the kids had all managed
to accumulate in about an hour's time. I thought back to the
massive amount of space Mother and I had in the Oktokraft,
which is really a bit of a dumb comment because the amount
of space in the Oktokraft was endless, and always would be,
no matter how much you packed in. Unfortunately, not so in
a Holden Station Wagon, a Morris 1000, and Mrs Lorelei's
Volkswagen. Never mind, no matter how much it hurt, we all
squeezed in with pleasure and optimism.

I was in the car with Mr Bleach, William, Sheila Nutter,
Kayleen MacNamara, Con, Umame and Oksana.

Sheila asked, "Mr Bleach, can you drop me back at school,
please? And Kayleen, take this. It's another radio-telephone
part that will connect us up wherever you'll be. I found it at
home; I remembered my dad had been in telecommunications
in the War. Lucky find!"

Mr Bleach made a cautious circuit around the school, and suggested the Canteen might be Sheila's safest 'office'. She agreed, hopped out and looked back in through the open window, saying, "Thanks Ek, thanks." She disappeared into the Westall night, past the block of classrooms to the Canteen. One flick of a bobby pin and whoosh, she was in. Grabbing a nutritious Wagon Wheel, she sat down at Mrs. DiCarlo's brown desk at the back, ready for action.

Even though Sheila had left Mr Bleach's car, it didn't seem like there was any extra space created for those left inside. Our bodies just blobbed out a bit more to fill up the holes, but it was still a long way from luxury.

"Why didn't you buy a Chevy?"

"Ever seen a teacher with a Chevy before?"

"No, but I've never seen a teacher go on a midnight mission with a pile of kids before either."

We both laughed. He was OK. A bit annoying, but OK.

As we drove off, I noticed we passed Coles and Ray, who tumbled out of Mrs Von Beethoven's car and swiftly ran to the front of the school before hiding in the nearest bushes. They seemed to be more than adequately equipped for any task.

"Well, where is Scout, then? She's meant to be here at school, too," commented Umame with some impatience. The other door swung open and, as the car backed up to drive off, we could see Scout slithering up the footpath like a hungry cobra, and into the caretaker's house, straight out of sight.

"Over the top," laughed Con.

"Oh really?" answered Umame, "I notice you're still sitting on your bum in the back of a comfy car."

Mr Bleach added, "So everyone's in place. What's our address then?"

"99 Kionga St, Clayton. That's where Maya Verdi lives," Con offered. "Not too far from Foodland!"

All three cars arrived at the address pretty much simultaneously, and the whole battalion of student warriors and liberators piled or fell out of their jails on wheels all at once.

"Ek! The lights are on. I can see one shining out that window."

"Well that's good news at least. I hope," answered Con. "Let's go check it out."

Anyone would swear that Con and Umame had seen The Guns of Navarone at least forty times by their approach to the building; their military style sidling, and their looks of communication to tell each other the coast was clear. The only manoeuvre that wasn't so clear was Umame's cartwheel that she performed near the back door.

In just a few minutes they were back.

Con spoke, "Ek, it's a bit spooky and quiet in there. There is definitely a light on inside."

"But we think it's the toilet," piped up Umame. "People don't normally spend their whole night in the toilet, do they?"

"Well, my Yiayia ate something off once that really did her guts in, and she—"

"Con please, we don't need to hear about her problems right now!"

I had to step in. "OK, guys. We believe there's nobody home just now. Take it away, Con and Umame. Dare to be different."

Umame spoke first. "Right, half of you come with me. We'll enter by the front door, and we'll look around the front rooms to see if there's anybody around."

Con added, "And my team will go by the back door and check out the back rooms."

"Yes," continued Umame, "Con is an expert in rooms at the back of the house, thanks to his Yiayia, so leave the one with the light on to him." She shrieked with laughter. Umame didn't think everything in life was funny really, but sometimes she felt so uncomfortable with herself that laughter seemed like the best option. There are some things that just are what they are, and so she left it at that.

"Time to move in, everyone, front and back. Take care, you're going into someone else's home."

On silent feet, our warriors entered the building, but by the time the teachers and I entered, the unanimous decision had been reached that the house was empty.

"Berenice," I said, "What exactly did the ambulance officer say to you again this morning?"

"That Maya would be home tonight."

"And now that you've had a chance to think, how did she look to you?"

"Well, very upset. Because of whatever it was she saw."

"Did she have any bruises or anything like that?"

"No, nothing."

"So is it possible your whole family went and picked her up from the hospital?"

"No. Two reasons. My mum's a nurse and I know you can't pick people up after 4.30 p.m., and also, Maya's grandpa is very sick, really very sick. He can't go out anywhere, and somebody always stays at home to look after him."

"Thank Berenice, and stay with us, because we're going to help you," I said. She looked so sad that my heart went out to her. William went one better, and stood right next to her.

Everyone was dead quiet when we realised we were very probably at the scene of some foul play. We all searched our minds for answers, no matter how small.

And it came. As I stood there thinking of the options, I casually raised my head and looked outside, approximately at the site of Umame's cartwheel. There, very briefly but very definitely and clearly, I saw the flash of a shimmer. It wasn't an everyday reflection shimmer, but the sort of shimmer that had shaped the whole of who I had become; the glimmer of a common identity. For a moment I stood, stock still, knowing exactly what I was looking at, but not really knowing what to do about it.

This was clearly a message, an indication that a solution to the disappearance of Maya and her family lay within my power to solve.

"I think I know what we have to do. I've seen a possible answer."

I looked around the room. Mr Bleach looked at me all too briefly, then looked away. I got the oddest feeling he might have seen it too.

A sea of confused faces met me. "We trust you, Ek," said William.

"We're going to the beach," I said.

While everyone was digesting this new direction, I drew away a bit, just to get some thinking space of my own for a few minutes. Without really being aware of it, I pulled out that treat that Mrs DiCarlo had given me; the Block in Bread.

"Hey Ek," chirped Kayleen as she noticed what I had in my

hand, "that's Canteen wrapping. What's in it?"

"Block in Bread," I replied.

"What's in it?"

"This stuff!"

"Do you know what that is, Ek?"

"Nah, I don't think so, Kayleen."

"It's cheese."

"Oh, OK. Thanks!"

Kayleen stood and examined me for a minute. "Ek, what's Gouda?"

"Um, not sure."

"Edam?"

"Nope."

"Maasdam, Beemster, Geitenkaas, Boerenkaas?"

I was beginning to feel a bit nervy with this barrage of words being thrown at me. "What are you trying to do, Kayleen?"

"You didn't know the stuff in your bread was cheese. All the words I chucked at you were types of cheese. You say you are Dutch, but the most important thing about Dutch, after clogs, is cheese, and you don't have a clue. Therefore, I can only conclude that you are not Dutch! So who are you, and where are you from?"

By the end of this tirade, Kayleen was pretty much screaming at me, and this had clearly caught the attention of the other students and the teachers.

I wanted to run, but I forced myself to confront these kids who deserved to know. Besides, who has ever run away because of a block of cheese, whatever that is.

"Everyone please, I have much to tell you, but before I do, I want you to know you are all very safe and I am here to help you. I have never wished for this moment to happen, but now I need to deal with it, and continue to help you as well. Before I start, let me please just say how much I care for, and respect you all." Slowly, William walked towards me and stood quietly on my right. A minute or so later, Mr Bleach stood on my left. I thanked them both, not really knowing what to do next.

Usually, when you have something important to say, it's usually best if you start by opening your mouth.

***

"Sheila here, Kayleen. Police, Armed Forces and Press on the oval awaiting further instructions. We know Dullard and Stipple are on the school grounds somewhere, but not yet located."

"Kayleen here Sheils. Maya and family have disappeared. Grandfather very ill. Oh, and I think Ek's an Alien!" and with

143

this comment she gave an uncertain chuckle.

***

I began to speak, although honestly I had no idea where things would head.

"All I ask is that you listen until I have completely finished, for this is probably the most difficult thing I've ever had to do." To be honest, everyone seemed shocked into listening to me, but I can't exactly say I had a rapt audience.

"My name is Prince Ek, the 74th and youngest son of King Ok and Queen Aggratenta, Supreme Beings of ULTERIATA BLACK HOLE GALAXY SUPERMASSIVATA. My world, my family and people, my society, have urged me to attend to a most urgent matter."

There was a distinct movement of interest as my story began to unfold.

"Only very recently, I learned that a group of holiday makers from our precious Black Hole fell upon a dreadful accident that caused their KruiseKraft to hurtle horribly into unknown directions, only to land in what we call 'The Blue-Green Planet', but which you call Earth; your Earth, your home. Our citizens fled as fast as they could into The Great Salt Pot, and you no doubt know where that is, but they were not safe at all."

Confusion, not knowing, and the unlikely horror of my revelation had brought the students to abject silence.

"Although my people had survived the dreadful accident that saw them stranded so many Okts away from home, the inhabitants of the planet started dredging them from the waters of The Great Salt Pot, dismembering their screaming bodies without the smallest concern, and burning them on greased metal plates, only to be torn to shreds by your families and friends to hungrily eat without a thought beyond their taste."

Everyone could see that I was struggling to hold back a tear.

"It's OK, Ek," said William, "we respect your right to speak, and we share your grief."

"Too right," said Con. "Personally, I'm disgusted. My family came from Greece. Just imagine if they'd been torn apart when their ship landed in Melbourne."

"Same for Oksana and me," said Umame, "only the Ukraine for us, of course. Well, don't look at me like that, Con. My dad was born there, but my mum's Japanese. Wanna make something of it?"

The kind but awkward chatter helped me control that insistent tear. 'Dare harder, Ek.'

"Thanks guys. I am here to take my lost friends back home, where they will finally be safe. So, why am I standing here with you? Well, this morning my Oktokraft was thrown, out of control and out of orbit, down onto your planet. We managed to land quite safely, but completely in the wrong place, behind your school in The Grange. My mother, the Queen, told me to get out and see what I could do to salvage the mission. I did just that, and hid my Kontrol Panel under some green spikes on the ground. My mother took off, but she is waiting for me on the dark side of the moon. Your friend Maya became involved in this totally by accident. We're all looking for her, and I'm looking for my fellow citizens as well. I ask you, please, please let's all continue to work together to help find them, and also attend to some of those dreadful matters back at your school."

At that point, I executed maximum energy. First, I had to ensure everyone's safety inside the house, but I also had to engineer a physical change so the students could see my true identity.

When I sensed the final moment had come, I gave one last push of energy. The entire space became lit with a huge dome of gold and ruby lanterns coming from my body. I realised I was at least twice the size I had been, and unending shimmers of light, like flowing waters, coursed through me. The students were, quite plainly, deeply moved by the vision I had become.

"Oh, Ek," gasped Umame.

"Amazing!" said Mrs Lorelei.

"And so peaceful," came Con.

I slowly lowered the energy movers that enabled me to show my alternative self until I was Ek the student again. I could sense that the students saw my dilemma as genuine, and we returned to being our old team again.

"Thank you," I said quietly, "and I won't stop until we find Maya and her family. I promise you."

CHAPTER 14.
DRAGNET

***

"KAYLEEN! STIPPLE AND DULLARD ARE located in the Woodwork Room. Forces alerted. Scout using Press to gain information on these two. Shouldn't be long."

"Thanks. Will let Umame and Con know."

"Really, an Alien? Crikey!"

"Yep. As real as Collingwood's crap!"

"Wow. That is real."

***

Kayleen rejoined the group. "Umame, Con, things are really hotting up back at school. Stipple and Dullard have been located, and we're expecting to move in very soon."

"OK, I'll go back," said Con, "I really want to be a part of this. I saw a bike around the back here. I'll borrow that. It'll take me no time. Good luck guys, and if we need to be in touch, we've got Sheila and Kayleen." And off he went.

Con's departure, however, did not settle the mood in the house.

"Well, Ek, what are we going to do now?" It was Margaret who raised this question. "Our school's flooded with hundreds of people in uniforms, chasing shady customers who are guilty of abuses and God knows what else; a Headmaster who can't cope anymore; we've got a whole family missing; a Bay full of traumatised octopuses, and an Alien who just dropped by and joined our class. Solution please, matey,"

***

"Sheila here, Kayleen. The Press people have been doing some research, hard as that is at night time. There are no records of Stipple and Dullard with the Ministry of Education. They are frauds. There is a trail, however, linking these two to a black-hearted organisation called 'The Revised Mind' that fights practically to the death to prevent children learning, thinking and advancing. Apparently our two aren't the only ones, but a number of other schools have also been infiltrated by this scum. It's just not clear yet which schools are infected by this group, but many are. One definite is the Hethersett College in Carnegie, and another the Sunshine School in Sassafras. Police and other Units are on their way to these schools as well. 'Operation Brain', they call it. Oh, and what does Ek look like, out of uniform?" she shrieked with laughter.

"Copy that Sheils. Thanks. Sounds like Scout's managing her area very well. I'm horrified about all that organisation stuff. We'll get them now. Oh, and very nice, really, for an Alien," she replied with a chuckle.

"What's with the 'copy that'?"

"Dunno. Saw it on TV."

Dullard and Stipple were sitting in the little office at the back of the Woodwork Room, about to embark on some rigorous worksheets and tests called "Mind Removal Tasks for Teenagers", and "Little People, Little Thought, Little Care!" The final project was called "Remove the Runts!"

"Oh Stip, our work is going somewhere. It's going to happen. Eventually we'll have our own chain of schools, with our specialised subjects."

"Yes, my darling, this is truly wonderful. Our life together is like an open highway."

There was a very sharp rap on the door.

"Right, you two! Get out of there!"

It was Coles and Ray, quietly followed by a platoon of expertly trained police.

"Ah, shut up you rotten little kids, before I cut your arms and legs off with a hacksaw," said Stipple.

"And I'll smooth out your ugly faces with some Number 12 sandpaper," added Dullard.

"Right, that's enough," said a burly police sergeant, "we're coming in!"

"Quick Stip, underground!" yelled Dullard, and they both

leaped towards the metal ring on the floor that they knew lead to the excess wood supply. Luckily, the ring had been quite well oiled by Mr Jack Lumbar, the Woodwork teacher, and the attached wooden panel easily lifted up so the two could climb down the stairs, shutting the panel behind them. It was seriously dark down there, but Stipple remembered he had a box of matches in his pocket. He quickly struck one and, not only was the cellar space lit up, but they could also see a long and deep corridor leading to goodness knows where. "Quick, this way," shouted Stipple, "there's a way out!"

Dullard realised she was caught on a nail along the wall, and it took quite a tug to release her, although she noticed her dress was slightly torn. As though the two had wings attached to their feet, they ran for some time until they reached another staircase out. Quick as a flash, they ascended, opened the latch outward, and felt the cool evening air, the same air that was inside the metal surround of the towering electricity pylon that lived in the school.

"Ah bum," spat Dullard, as she realised they had graduated from a wooden cage to a metal one. All around them were the powerful beams of hundreds of torches. They couldn't work out the exact uniforms, but they could distinguish there were different types. This was certainly a major operation in their honour.

"We've got to get out, Stip. Throw something over the wires to knock out the power!" Stip looked around for a while, then he took off the furry style shoes that the students had always made fun of, when they would ask if he was wearing his pet raccoon.

He tied both laces together, and attached the untied ends, one to each shoe. This left him with some sort of hurtling device. He twirled it around his head about ten times—narrowly missing Dullard to her disgust—and then threw it right up to the wires. For a pretend P.E. teacher, that was pretty amazing, as the created catapult fell perfectly across two wires. There was a huge flash of light, and then a blackout. The school, the street, the entire suburb and more were in darkness, apart from the torches carried by the Forces, which looked pathetically weak.

"Where are they?"

"Can't see them. Just vanished."

"Unbelievable!"

"Hey, no!" shouted Con. "There they are. On the pylon!"

Sure enough, the two were clambering to the top of the pylon, but nobody could imagine where they'd go from there.

"Get down, you two. You can't get away. You're trapped and we're waiting down here to take you into custody! Get down or settle for the consequences!" Con always had such a great way with words. Subtle.

Trapped but not totally lost, Dullard slid herself onto one of the wires, swinging from arm to arm across, hopefully, to the other side. Stipple watched and copied her idea, and there they were, swinging from tree to tree like two great apes. When they had moved about eight or ten arm spans across, Dullard suddenly started twitching. It seemed that the little cut in her dress, that she had earlier caught on a nail, suddenly began unraveling at some speed, causing Dullard herself to slip off the wire. The crocheted green dress was her only hope and she tied the loose end to the cable above. She'd have to let go. Either the uncoiling of the thread would hold her hanging there, or she would shatter down onto the ground below. Release! She spun down quite a distance, but when her screaming reached a peak, her downward spiral suddenly ended with a sudden jerk, and she dangled, suspended, like a spider in her own web.

Stipple tried to force himself past the unfortunate Dullard, and while trying to dodge the thread of doom, he noticed something fall out of his pocket. "Damn," he thought, "let's hope they don't notice."

The hanging spider and her mate were suddenly lit up by a few hundred torches.

"You two. Get down here. Your stinking nasty little game is up, and if you're not down in ten seconds, let me just remind you we have high pressure hoses here to help you down. Coles and Ray, they're all yours!"

"Three, two, one, water!" shouted Coles and Ray. The effect was like trying to survive being in a waterfall. Rivers, no, oceans of water seemed to pour over them. They had to make a move before they drowned.

"That's it, get yourselves back the way you came. Give them a helping hand, Officers. Double the water pressure!"

A gagging and choking pair was met at the base of the pylon,

Stipple in bare feet, and Dullard in, well, somewhat less than what she started the day with—much less in fact.

One police officer came running with something in his hand.

***

"Sheila here, Kayleen. Spider Woman and Ape Man are being arrested as we speak. Great credit to Coles, Ray and Con. Just waiting on Scout now to do interview. We're on a roll."

"Excellent, Sheila. Lots happening here too. Just short of one link to get us moving. Hang on a tick. What's that? OK, I'll tell her. Sorry Sheila, that was Umame. She just asked if you could arrange complete public road closures between Westall and The Mornington Peninsula, with all personnel ready to relocate rapidly if necessary."

"Sounds good, Kayleen, consider it done."

***

Margaret came forward, quite excited and a bit flustered, really. "Umame, Ek, I was thinking. Considering there is absolutely nothing in this house, nothing at all that could be traceable to anyone, do you think it might be, um, well there's a possibility, er, I found this."

She held up a sheet of paper, like a mini poster, that had some information printed on it. She read aloud:

"Is your child getting too big for his boots?

Does he ask too many questions, as if you care.

Does she get off on knowledge and learning?

Would you like to dispose of them?

Fortnightly lectures, 'Control the Child in your Child.' Satisfaction guaranteed.

Reasonable Rates.

Drinks at Bar Prices.

Bali Ahoy Senior Social Club."

This definitely looked like a possible clue.

"Thanks, Fingers," Umame said to Margaret. "Hey guys, we need all your brains for a minute. Margaret just found this flier lying around the house." She read it to all and they were pretty amazed.

"We need to know where this place is. It's certainly a mystery."

Everyone agreed it was a serious mystery, until Mrs Von Beethoven popped her head around the corner. "Ha! You young people, honestly, you crumble at the drop of a little poster. As soon as I heard you read that, I ran out to get"—and she was clearly over excited by her great thought—"my Melways!"

Groans all around, but Mrs Von Beethoven got straight to work. "Let me see, Social Clubs, um, 'Avocado Lovers Social Club', 'Bad Food Social Club', here we are, 'Bali Ahoy Senior

Social Club'. Map 101, Mount Eliza. Here we go, and here it is, and it is right next door to Where the Florist Meets the Sea. Easy to find. No, don't thank me, no need."

Unfortunately, as soon as everyone started cheering Mrs Von Beethoven's work, the phone rang, and Kayleen indicated she might like to hear.

"Sheila here. Something for you. Stipple dropped something out of his pocket. A box of matches. The top reads, Bali Ahoy Senior Social Club."

"Fantastic Sheila, and I've got something for you too. Margaret found a poster in May's house. It says, Bali Ahoy Senior Social Club. Now isn't that a coincidence?"

"Snap!" countered Sheila. "Now, Con, Umame, all others, close the dragnet. We'll soon be able to kill two birds with one stone, I suspect. Oh and Ek, how are you going? Don't forget you're not alone. You are not alone."

I loved this place so much, I had almost forgotten what alone was.

Closing the dragnet might have sounded like a simple instruction from a recipe, but in reality it constituted a huge operation. First, we had to ensure a straight and safe run from Westall High School to where the Bali Ahoy Social Club was, in Mt Eliza, and these two places were quite a long distance apart. The little town of Westall wasn't at all glamorous or showy, but it brimmed with life and activity. Mt Eliza, on the other hand, was like an extremely good looking person with no brain. At first you'd be hypnotised by the looks, but then quickly bored to death from the lack of a working mind.

Not only did we need to secure an unimpeded route between these two places, but we still had to keep safe and easy access for ambulances, firefighters and the like. It was decided to secure the road in total, then have aerial support to indicate where emergency openings needed to be put in place. The police would stay in Westall in case anything flared up there, the army would work from Mentone to Frankston, while the Air Force would do ongoing runs all the way through to Mt Eliza.

***

A volunteer helicopter pilot approached the Air Command.

"Commander, I've flown helicopters around the world, and I'm very keen to help these young people in their difficult, but vital mission."

"What about him?" the Commander queried.

"Well, Air Commodore, wherever I go, he goes."

"Very well. As you were. Pleasant journey. The Lieutenant will also accompany you. A question of Regulations only. Ten-Four!"

And so the mystery helicopter assumed its place in the take-off queue and they finally departed.

***

"Sheila, Westall here, now connected to all forces. Route South closure now underway along Nepean Highway. Note preparation for emergency routes beyond general plan; at Frankston Hospital, Carrum Swamp and Morning Star Home for Delinquent Boys. Good luck everyone!

***

Scout felt a little flustered at the rate with which other areas of the mission were proceeding. She clasped the magical little box of matches that had given them such a huge leap ahead in their investigations.

"We need some solutions," she said to herself.

"Con, how do you want to organise this? I've got about thirty press people waiting to write this up, and then there's these two, Stipple and Dullard."

"Well, I reckon we'll put the two over there, with their backs against the pylon so the Press can take photos. I don't think the Press will mind sitting on the grass."

"Great idea for a Form 1 kid, Con," said Scout playfully, "Um, Officers, would you mind bringing the Dynamic Duo over here? Have they dried off a bit yet? Yes, just in front of the pylon here. No, I don't think handcuffs will be necessary. Where could they possibly go?"

"OK, Scout, it's your show," said Con, who loved dramatic talk. "Roll 'em!"

"Con, why is this school so full of dags?" asked Scout, laughing.

"Right, here we go, ladies and gentlemen of the Press. We have uncovered in our school, and elsewhere, a cell of terror operatives whose role it is to wipe out school students. These two behind me, these two terrible, unforgivably horrible people have been uncovered and arrested following a series of unthinkable and cruel acts against the students here. Do you have any questions you'd like to ask these two?"

"What's wrong with kids?"

"Mine love school and work really hard."

"They've even got favourite teachers!"

"How are kids supposed to get anywhere without schools and great teachers?"

"Well, that's a fair start," said Scout. Turning behind her, she asked, "And your answers?"

Dullard went first. "Kids make me sick, it's as though they think they really have the right to have their opinions heard the whole time, to participate, to join in, to have a say. Well, vomit to that I say. Irritating children make my flesh crawl. They're gutless, they're lazy, they're inattentive, and the whole purpose of dragging them into brainless holes like this one is ridiculous. It's a huge drain on our taxes, not to mention our fine brains."

Then Stipple added, "Yeah, whatever she said."

"So you've formed an international organisation to wipe out students?" said a local journalist from The Oakleigh Standard.

"So what? We haven't done anything wrong."

Just then, a familiar figure stepped around the corner, along with Sheila, our Director of Communications.

"Forgive me, everyone," Sheila began, "before I pass you on to a most significant speaker in this regard, I just wanted to add a few nuts and bolts points myself: like when you sat outside our classroom in your car, and that was meant to be supervision: like when you left classes by themselves for hours at a time: like when you slammed doors in kids' faces and on their fingers: like when you stuck your dirty great bare feet on my desk: like when you ignored children whose families had come from other countries: like when you ignored girls when they wanted to answer a question—yes even you, Dullard: like the total air of contempt and disregard that you breathed over us all." Sheila had found her strength and never missed a beat.

The Press seemed visibly overwhelmed by this passionate plea from a student. They wrote and tapped furiously on their type-writers, not wanting to fall behind.

The man who had been waiting patiently next to Sheila moved forward.

"My name is Frank Glass. I am the Principal of Westall High School. Stipple and Dullard, hear this. When you first came to this school at the start of the year, I welcomed you as two young people new to the profession. I saw that, at times, you were prone to severe methods. When I spoke to you about these, you said you were representatives of the Ministry of Education, and that I would be expected to do whatever the Ministry had dictated. I watched myself growing more and more narrow, nastier, more cruel, and less open to what I had always admired—an openness and friendliness between all parties in a school. Thanks to your vicious demand and prodding, I became a tyrant, unable to reclaim who I wanted to be, because I thought this had all come from the Ministry. And then, when I thought things couldn't go any further, you told me, Miss Dullard, that my own two children had been kidnapped. I snapped in two at that point, unable to move, unable to think. And it was just a lie to make me crack even further. At least I know you two have been caught. You disgust me. I only have one more thing to add: this afternoon I resigned my position as Headmaster of this school. I also apologise for all the things I did so horribly wrong."

A respectful silence fell over the crowd, endlessly recording every detail he put forward, and also reflecting on all that must have gone on in this place.

In the middle of this serenity and thoughtfulness, Stipple and Dullard suddenly looked at each other, nodded, and made a dash for it. They jumped the fence behind the pylon, then looked back at the crowd and screamed, "We'll see you all in hell, you pathetic losers!" With that, they ran in opposite directions to each other. Dullard clearly had a black bike pre-planted in a bush, and she peddled frantically towards The Grange. Stipple, on the other hand, had organised himself with a sleek motorbike, and he tore past the school at what sounded like about three-hundred kilometres per hour.

The assembled crowd, and even the Police Officers, had been so moved by the passionate cries of Sheila and Mr Glass, that they had carelessly stopped concentrating on the two who should have been watched more closely than anyone.

***

"Sheila To Kayleen, Crochet alert! Dullard and Stipple escaped. Suspected route south to Mt Eliza."

"Well, bugger!"

"Agreed."

***

CHAPTER 15.
CARRUM SWAMP

***

"ATTENTION ATTENTION. ALL FORCES ATTENTION!"

"Yes, I'm here, Sheila," said Kayleen.

"Look we all need to make a move, Kayleen. Our work at Westall is done just now, and I don't think you're going to find Maya and her family where you're standing either. Next stop is the Bali Ahoy Senior Social Club, but we don't know how safe that is as yet, and my guess is Tweedledum and Tweedledee on his motorbike will be heading there too. Let's meet up at the Carrum Swamp, OK?"

"Sounds posh, eh?"

"Yeah, not exactly The Grange! See you there!"

***

In both of the major operational sites, frantic action stirred to locate and apprehend Dullard and Stipple, find Maya and her family, and rescue my people from the ugly fates they had been suffering.

"Right," I said, having found my confident voice again, "we need to regroup. Kayleen, please ask Sheila to dismantle the Westall High School operation as she sees fit, and also determine the best action for the Forces to take. Con and Umame can then ensure their best practice and communications with us. You can do the same at Maya's house. I suggest if we all leave in about half an hour, then that should give us plenty of exit time."

"I don't think we should all move together, just in case something confronts us along the way," Kayleen said. "Hey, Ek the Alien, where are we going exactly? What's our target destination?"

"The Carrum Swamp," I said, as if I'd known this all along.

"Hear that, Sheils?"

"Sure thing! Carrum Swamp. Sounds classy!"

'Next round,' I thought to myself. It seemed remarkable how one decision seemed to flow naturally from another. It wasn't about some inner gift as I had suspected and feared; it was about being practical, and logical.

"Pack the cars," I said.

"Pack the cars!" Kayleen said.

"Pack the cars!" Con said to Umame.

"Pack them yourself!" Umame laughed back at Con, so we all decided that it might be faster if we all just packed the cars instead of bossing everyone else around.

In no time we were ready to roll, and we presumed the other

group were also on the road.

It was clear that Sheila had made adjustments to the police presence along the roadway. Every one or two kilometres there appeared to be a wayside check to see if we were OK. We learned that Sheila's party were somewhere ahead of us, and so we continued. The road lights had been completely turned off. The only untoward traffic that might break through this net of control would be a giant moth on roller skates or Dullard and Stipple trying to do some more damage.

A flash of lights lit up the sky, and a cordon of some fifty heli-copters was shooting up ahead, weaving in and out of each other like an unbreakable wall. Their weaving, both horizon-tally and vertically, reminded me of the seven planets we had encountered on our way here, thundering through space, but in a formation so tight that it seemed almost impossible. That vision seemed so very long ago. So much had happened since then.

The Nepean Highway, our main avenue of travel, became darker and darker, and it seemed as though the police patrols were fewer in number. This Carrum Swamp was clearly a very isolated spot, leading us to goodness knows what further discoveries.

All at once, all our cars began sliding along the road; not just little slips, but huge slippery diversions from one side of the road to the other. At one point, Mrs. Von Beethoven's Volk-swagen made a complete, full circle turn. Certainly there was much panic in all the cars.

"What's going on?"

"There's stuff on the road!"

"Somebody's thrown stuff!"

"Watch out!"

"Slow down so we can see what it is!"

Well, that seemed like a slightly practical solution, so our patient driver, Mr Bleach, slowed the Station Wagon and wound the windows down.

"They're giant snakes," he said with some fear in his voice, "and they're longer than the whole road from one side to the other."

"Give me a gander," suggested Con, "oh good lord, you guys, hopeless! Sorry Mr Bleach, but you are. I come here every year with my dad and sister. We're just off Eel Race Road. These are eels, they can travel across land to find different water pools. It's like going on a holiday for them. So go easy driving along. You don't want to hurt them."

"Strange you didn't know about them, Mr Bleach," said Kayleen.

"Yeah, I know," said Bleach, "I'm from Perth originally. It's way too hot for eels there," he said, without sounding at all like he knew what he was talking about.

"Hey, wind up all the windows quick. Eels can travel straight up. They're probably right near the windows already." Sure enough, eel faces began to appear, so some very quick handle turning ensured they were kept outside of the car. We noticed the others do the same, as well as someone screaming hysterically in the third car.

"That's Mrs Lorelei," said Con.

"Yeah, how funny is she?" answered Umame.

After driving very slowly past the eel highway, I did have a feeling that we were definitely heading in the right direction, for a whole lot of things.

It wasn't long before two police officers flagged us down.

"Good evening, all. I'm Inspector Ash Pendale, and this is Sergeant Pat Lakes. Just behind us, well, it's a bit obscured at the moment to avoid unwanted onlookers, is the Gateway to The Carrum Swamp. Miss Sheila from Communications Control alerted us to your arrival. We'll enable your entry and then close the barricade behind you. Take care in there. It's a darn creepy place, so if you need anything at all, just shout."

"Don't worry, Inspector, there's someone in the car in front who's an expert in shouting. Would you like some help clearing the entrance barricade? Come on guys, let's give the officers a hand."

Everyone jumped out of the cars. This was the most complex web of twigs, branches, rocks, fake giant spiders and plastic owls imaginable, and I imagined it would put off even the worst offender. But Stipple and Dullard?

The officers thanked us heartily, as we ventured into the deepest recesses of The Carrum Swamp. After a few minutes, we hit upon what looked like some houses, but on closer inspection it became clear that they were a group of treehouses. Actually, more than a group, they were clearly a system of treehouses, with connecting doors and stairs and latches, and linking passageways, tunnels, roof shelters and joined chimneys that were actually huge living spaces.

It really was very difficult to see much detail, and everyone's little domestic torches were not enough to cast some clear light on the whole, gloomy scene.

Kayleen being Kayleen, suggested, "Hey Ek, why don't you light yourself up again, like you did in Maya's place. Then we'll be able to see."

"Thanks Kayleen, that's a bit like me suggesting you wear your pyjamas to the school assembly."

"Ek, sometimes, well a lot of the time really, you can be such a drag! Hey everybody, not all of you have seen this, but Ek's got this really cool party trick where he can light himself up, without fire even. Show 'em, Ek!"

Of course, the encouraging shouting and egging started, and there was no way out.

"Better call the Fire Brigade, Kayleen," and just as everyone started laughing—Whoosh! The shimmering reality looked even more marvellous out in the open, as gasps of disbelief and respect filled the space. They could see I wasn't just a light, but a being that could give off light."

Pymble Welsh stepped forward and thanked me. "Don't just stare at him, please. He didn't just do this to be an ornament. Now, I've noticed there are four main sections to this 'house' space. We need to explore each. Communications Officers, Group Leaders, Individual Thinkers, let's regroup and work systematically through this hole of a place."

Sheila immediately stepped forward. "Absolutely correct, Pymble, and let's get going. Find your group, and have the eyes of a microscope." She turned again to Pymble and said, "You're the best, Pymble."

Lit up by my Beacon, the teams set forth to try and discover what this creepy place might reveal. They had to wind themselves up and around gnarled branches, some with twenty centimetre spikes bent outward to reject unwelcome visitors. In front of one door there was a barely disguised trapdoor to quickly remove any trespasser from areas where something 'of interest' might be found.

Con's group thought they'd entered a house of horrors, once they got past a series of nasty obstacles designed to keep them out. On a long, metal table, they saw a whole array of chains, and locks, and ropes, clearly a collection of tools to keep people restrained. Children perhaps? People who work for the good of children? This space was like a sickening torture chamber.

Luckily I, Ek 'Beacon', was able to see everything from my height advantage. You know, I could never have imagined such places existed. What had twisted people's minds to such an extent that they even need these. This second space was dingy like the first, but filled with thousands of bottles either stuffed with disease-looking liquids in all possible vile colours, or full of bits of animal: dog paws, kitten tails, snakes and massive spiders; another section labelled 'Deadly Poisons' and, at the back, in a very large glass like a screw-topped tub, I could see what I feared most, a viciously, crudely hacked octopus. I could not move. I was so terrified by what I saw, and at the same time so angry that every part of me was seething with fury.

I stood frozen like this for some time, when I heard someone below say, "It's Ek. He's crying." Not long after that, I don't really know how long, I was aware of Mr Bleach next to me.

"Ek, it's because of bastards like this that you're on this mission. Don't lose your power. You have great power, and we will help you. I will help you. Come on down, you deserve a break."

I went and sat on a log, slowly allowing my lights to wear thin. "Thanks, Bleach," I said. "You're OK." We sat together for a while.

"Ek! Mr Bleach! Look what I've found!" It was Margaret, and as she ran towards me, at least seven or eight ran behind her to see what her great find was.

"Margaret," said Mr Bleach, "hold it up high so we can see your discovery."

So she did. She held it up. She raised it up higher, and when everyone's eyes were fully on it, there was a communal "Ooh! Ooh! Well there's proof all right!"

"Yes, here's proof. It's green, it's a thread, it's for making clothes— it's some of the thread used to make Dullard's disgusting dress."

"So this is really Stipple and Dullard's home," I said, "Disgusting. Doesn't surprise me one bit. I want you to remove every shred of evidence that this place ever existed. Don't overlook anything. Go to it, everyone, except Margaret, there's a special job for you."

So, they scrubbed and removed and polished and waxed and vitalised and whatever else it took to make a massive horror home disappear. At last they were all done and sat around with Bleach and me.

"Now Margaret, we'll get up from this log, and there are a few nice things in the bag here that need to be arranged as a lovely welcome home gift for Stipple and Dullard."

Margaret picked up the bag and, after some time thinking, creating and designing, she artistically placed these items on the log: a vase of flowers, a photo of Mr Glass, and one of Stipple's furry shoes with an extra green shoelace.

Home Sweet Home. If they ever get back.

CHAPTER 16.
BALI AHOY

***

"PILOT TO CO-PILOT. PILOT TO Co-Pilot. Roger! Roger!"

"Co-Pilot to Pilot. Co-Pilot to Pilot. Why are we saying all this stuff Mum?"

"What do you mean, Bobby?"

"Well, we're sitting right next to each other. Who else do you think I'm going to be talking to?"

"Oh yeah, sorry. Hey, have you spotted them?"

"Yep, just down there. Not far from the City Centre. And I bet they're not thinking of doing a spot of shopping in Myers. That's always a bit hard when it's shut."

"Let's keep a close eye on them so we don't lose them between the city buildings. I'm intrigued to know where they're going. It's the opposite direction from everyone else."

"Yeah, I know, but I'll be a koala's chance at the Melbourne Cup if we don't reel them in when we know where they're going."

"A koala's what? Did you just make that up Bobby?

"Yep. It's my latest. Like it?"

"I don't think it's ready for the dictionary yet."

"Hey, how funny was it?"

"How funny was what? Who?"

"The sign, Mum! You know, the sign in the restaurant, and Ek said ice cream! I'll be laughing at that for the next ten years. What a joke!"

"Yeah, you got him a beauty, Co-Pilot."

"Pardon? What do you mean 'Co-Pilot'?"

"Haha, got you too, Pilot! And you know what?"

"What?"

"I'm very proud of you, Bobby!"

"Thanks, Mum, you're pretty groovy yourself. One thing though."

"What?"

"I can't see the motorbike. Kidding!"

***

Inspector Pendale joined the cavalcade of students, teachers and an unusual glowing thing that he had observed through the dense woodland, just to make sure they were all safe. Sergeant Lakes would stay to man the 'Gates to Hell', as the two officers called the place, and that was even before the Westall team took to clearing out the vile contents they had uncovered. The two seasoned police officers had experienced some grim sights in their careers, and as fathers and grandfathers, they were sickened by what the two inhabitants of the tree houses had in mind. Such are all societies, in which the scummiest subculturals can coexist with those who really try to take care of others, and value fairness, safety and justice. At least, that's what our two officers of the law believed.

"See ya, Ash."

"Onya, Pat."

And once again they were off. The distance from Carrum to Mt Eliza isn't normally very long or difficult, but it was obvious our caravan of cars was harbouring some tiring passengers. The problem was, though, that they all knew they couldn't really afford luxuries like tiredness. There was so much still to be achieved.

From Carrum, they cautiously entered the precinct of Seaford. They could clearly hear the lapping of small waves from the Bay's waters on the right.

"This is that Giant Salt Liquid Pot," I said to my fellow travellers, sadly. "All of it. I can sense the distant crying of my people. At last someone is on the way to help them. I so hope we can help."

"Don't worry, Ek," said Umame, "We'll all do our very best. The hard thing is right now, when we don't really know what 'very best' needs to look like."

"Well, you can't say we don't have imagination."

After Seaford came Frankston, and we seemed to slip into a side road, travelling higher, ever higher, until we could turn our cars toward the water. We quickly parked the cars for a brief plan of action.

Sheila addressed us all, "You'll notice we're pretty high up, and this place is called Oliver's Hill. Now, unlikely, but if anyone gets lost, you must make your way back here. It's our safe spot. Don't forget, we don't know where Stipple and Dullard are right now, and we don't know how many of their disgusting cronies are a part of this Bali Ahoy business. Furthermore, we'll be pretty much out in the open helping Ek save his friends, so we're easy pickings. Stay close, and we should all be OK."

Con came forward.

"I don't want to raise any false concerns, but where's Bobby?"

There was a sudden realisation that it had been some time since he'd been seen.

"It's because we've all been travelling in different cars," said Kayleen. "It's been ages since I've seen him. He certainly wasn't in Maya's house. Who saw him at school?"

To stop any further growing anxiety, Inspector Pendale immediately made Police contact to raise an alert of the highest order, to effect the tracing of Bobby; he emphasised that the boy might be in considerable danger, and all State Personnel needed to be on the lookout as from this second.

Of course, none of the State Personnel thought to look up, high above where they expected the action to be, at a rather large helicopter weaving its way through the skies, as if it was following and chasing something, rather like a giant dragonfly after a blowfly.

***

"There they go, Mum," screamed Bobby, "Stipple and Dullard are heading past Werribee! You know what they're doing, don't you? They're not going the wrong way, they're going the 'other' way."

"Gotcha, Bobby, well done. They're planning to go right around the Bay to get to The Bali Ahoy. Let's cut them off at the pass and create some disappointing moments for them."

"Cut them off at the pass? Mum, what film did you pick that line up from? Ha! Cut them off at the pass?"

"Look, do you want to wash restaurant dishes for the next eight years?"

"What do you mean, Mum? Cut them off at the pass—did you know that's my favourite saying? So clever!"

"Yeah, yeah, right. Hey, look Bobby, they're on the road to Geelong. We'll swing left across the water. Watch out you two, this town ain't big enough for the four of us."

"I think it's tablet time, Mum."

***

Sheila continued, "I understand that our deepest thoughts, and maybe even fears, are with Bobby, but we need to move on to achieve our other goals. We can't just fall in a heap now."

"That's right, Sheila," said Umame, "we're really not very far from our destination. It's just a couple of kilometres on our right. There's a bit of a street from this Highway down to the Club and the beach. We'll need to unpack everything as soon as we have turned into the street from the Highway, then make our way to the Club on foot."

"Thanks, Umame," said Con. "There's so much luggage to take down to the beach, it's going to be a bit of a tiring trek. Take your time, work in teams and share the load. We need you active and energised at the other end. Good luck! You ready to roll, Pymble?"

"Sure am. Special agent Pymble Welsh reporting for duty, Sir!"

"Excellent! Back in the cars!"

Anticipation always makes time last longer than it actually is, and so it was that a humble two or three kilometres seemed to go for hours.

"Turn right, Garish Grove, this is it."

As though all the car wheels had been endowed with velvet

slippers, the cars slid silently into the side of the road. Everyone bounced out with renewed energy, although the thought of Bobby was, of course, never very far from our minds. Unpacking was systematic and disciplined, in order of need. Everyone knew instinctively what to do, because that's the way kids are. They don't wait around for titles, promotions and salary increases, they just see a job to be done and know what they have to do.

"Right, let me just do a little run around the cars to make sure we've got everything."

"Margaret, you go left first," suggested Berenice, "and I'll circle round from the right."

"And we'll crash in the middle." They both laughed. It was good to see Berenice laugh a bit. "We better find Maya."

And so the long march began. While there was quite a lot of luggage, the evening itself was quite splendid. I looked up and saw how high the dome of the sky was, and how beautiful. There were only a few wispy clouds and a thin slice of moon.

"There's Mother," I said to myself. I didn't really know what else to think, or expect when that time came. In just one day on this Blue-Green Planet, I had experienced many wonderful feelings and endless laughter, better than any single day of my life back on ULTERIATA BLACK HOLE GALAXY SUPERMASSIVATA.

"Come on Ek, pull it together. There's too much to do right now," came Pymble's voice.

Closer and closer we trudged to the end of Garish Grove.

"Everybody listen," whispered Pymble, "in a minute I'm going to creep up to the Bali Ahoy Senior Social Club at the end of the street to have a bit of a look around. If it's closed for the evening then it'll be plain sailing, but if not, I'll come and get you all. Just in case, I need someone to go next door to the shop called 'Where the Florist Meets the Sea', and 'borrow' a pile of prickly cactus stalks. Inspector Pendale, I'd like you to be on standby as well, if possible."

"Always son, no worries."

And so Pymble disappeared into the darkness. He was pretty much a city kid, so it surprised us how much he enjoyed the freshness of the air blowing onto the land from the sea. He also felt as though he was bathing in the openness of nature, as though it carried him along, almost weightless. He could see a twinkling of lights coming from the building up ahead. That answered his main question. The place was full of people. He crept close enough to be able to peek through a small window at the side.

"Oh my great heavens," whispered Pymble to himself. The vision that met him from inside was something he had never encountered before. There were about forty or fifty people inside—over-dressed, over-jewelled and seriously over-wrinkled—with purple stringy lips, endless earlobes weighed down and torn open by really heavy diamonds, and sacks of papery skin dangling from under the hems of some very expensive dresses. Their eyes looked like flat tractor tyres, and their noses were overly long, like used drainpipes. And they did a dance, some sort of thumping dance restricted by joints that hadn't budged for at least seventy years; slow, so pathetically slow, yet so grimly determined.

Pymble knew the tune from the pounding on the ivories, executed by an equally age-challenged gent on an oxygen tank. The Mexican Hat Dance it was, but dragged down to such a pathetic pace that it could have been a terrific version of the Funeral March.

"Da…dum…da…dum…da…dum……da…did…dle…dee…die…. No! Don't die you lot," he whispered, as he suddenly spotted something hanging from the wall on the other side. "You've got a lot to answer for!" Pymble slowly slid down the outside wall and sped back along the road.

Back at the cars, and panting, he breathlessly explained, "They're in all right. Horrible, repulsive people. But that's not the worst. There's a sign on the wall."

"What does it say?" they all asked at once.

"It says, 'YOUNG PEOPLE ARE THE PROBLEM. GET THEM!'"

"Any sign of Stipple?"

"Or Dullard?"

"Or Maya?"

A thousand questions were thrown in Pymble's direction, but of course he didn't have the answers. He had a plan, though.

"Did someone go to the flower shop next door?"

"Yeah, I went," said Oksana, "and I took Mr Bleach with me in case there was too much to carry. It's all ready to go."

"Great," enthused Pymble, "it's time to move. Everything and everyone needs to come with us. When we get to the front of the Bali Ahoy Senior Social Club, put everything down, then I'll instruct you all on what to do next. Now, let's go."

I watched Pymble at work; I could see he was a rare gem and, by the looks of admiration he received, the others thought so too.

After an arduous twenty minutes or so of carrying, hauling and dragging ourselves along the road, we arrived at The Bali Ahoy Senior Social Club. We unpacked our piles of goods as systematically as before, and Pymble called us all together, but very quietly of course.

"Inspector Pendale and Mrs Von Beethoven, I'd like you both to be at the front of the line with me. Everyone else, please make a line. Everyone is to carry a stem of cactus. I know you guys all work best when you respond to the moment, so keep your eyes peeled, understand what's going on and take your part. Let's go! Me and Mrs Von Beethoven first, then you, Inspector. Feel the moment."

"Right you are, son," Pendale replied, not really knowing what that would feel like.

Mrs Von Beethoven and Pymble walked up to the front door and rang one of those clangy little things that are a poor excuse for a resounding bell. The Mexican Hat Dance ended abruptly, and the shuffling of many painful feet was heard nearing the door. After some awful creaking, from the inmates' bones and not the door, the latter opened.

"Hi there. We're the act that was booked for tonight."

"Oh well, we don't know about that," said some fellow whose trousers appeared to be distinctly moist, "I—"

"Well, I'm sure you do know, Mr. What's your name again?"

"Heckle," he said.

"Exactly," said Mrs Von Beethoven. "You're the man I spoke to."

"Mum," said Pymble to Mrs Von Beethoven, "it's getting a bit chilly. Can we go in now?"

Inspector Pendale pushed himself forward. "Is there some sort of problem here? These people have booked. You've forgotten. I'm a Police Inspector and these two are my wife and son. I suggest you add all that up. Need a minute? No worries. Right then."

"Just stand wherever you like, and our act will work around you," instructed Pymble.

Mrs Von Beethoven threw herself into action the second she got in the door. "Ladies and Gentlemen, we thank you so very much inviting our company, 'Legs 'n' Vocals', to perform for you tonight. And here they are with their opening number, 'Let The Ocean Wild!'"

Pymble ran into the large performance space with, to the surprise of everyone, a huge, fantastic voice; not your average, run of the mill good voice, but one of those voices that's wrapped in gold leaf.

"The sea is not an ocean, and the ocean is not a sea … ." His notes were totally pure; this boy was a star. As he started to "ooh" and "aah", Mrs Von Beethoven took up the words to Pymble's backing. One by one, the others entered the club, each adding to the effect of a massive and brilliant vocal act. Each time Pymble started a new theme, others would immediately pick it up, just like they'd learned at The Chow Palace. The sound was astonishing, perfect. On the other hand, the Old Folk, the child haters, looked like they were going to be sick.

When Pymble saw their reaction, he lifted his cactus stem as a sign to act. While still singing, he now began to dance around the repulsive child haters. Everyone quickly joined in, dancing behind Pymble, making the circle tighter by prodding the offending oldies with all the cactus stems, until the whole group had wound itself in a tight circular knot. Pymble led the chorus in a spectacular finish, and silence fell over the room.

He said, "Because of you, some of our friends are missing."

He could see there was no pity on their faces, so he said, "And now we will perform, 'The Maya Song.' Put your hands together everyone, for Ek Van Ok; the Golden Voice, the Silver Tonsils, the Brass Bellows, all the way from Dutch!"

I stepped to the front to assist with my energies, and began the glow of my other body that my Westall High School friends now knew so well. At once they broke out with "Ekekekekekekekekekekek!"

They braced themselves for the exquisite sounds that would come forth. Would this really bring Maya back? The humming started in layers, working up in energy. It was again so totally beautiful. I looked at the faces of the child haters, and I saw only cold, immovable concrete. Into the humming chant, I began to blend in the name Maya, Maya, a hundred and one times, until I indicated an immediate lowering of volume. This allowed other sounds to come in, the waves, the wind.

And then, so soft and frightened, we heard,

"Berenice, it's me, Maya. I'm under the building. Please come!"

Like an avalanche, the kids ran outside to find Maya, at long last. I stayed with Inspector Pendale. "Great work, son, and well done. And where did you get that amazing octopus outfit? So realistic, especially the tentacles."

"Thank you, but they're Arms really."

"Ah well, there you go. Still excellent."

Lucky thing a busload of police reinforcements had just arrived. "In here, Constables. You can take this lot to the Morning Star Bad Boys Home to cool off for a while. They probably have space for a few bad girls too. Be careful they don't snap though. We want them alive and well in the courtroom."

A sudden bustle occurred at the door, and there was the best sight ever—Maya, her parents and her grandfather, all glowing with appreciation.

"Thank you, everyone," said Maya. "It's seemed like such a long time, but we're OK now. We're all OK. I think my parents and Grandpa might like a relaxing seat on the balcony with something nice to eat, like a veggie burger, and a drink. He likes a large glass of stout. But Berenice, I'd like to be with all of you though. You've all done so much for me, and I know there's work to be done now."

Umame came forward. "I would just like to ask Pymble where he learned to sing and dance like that. You were … outstanding! Maybe, just maybe I thought we shouldn't bother going back to school, well, ever again, really. Then we can just do world tours and stuff with you and this amazing act. What do you say, Pymble?"

"Thanks Umame, but I'm on telly every Saturday afternoon. I'm on Brian and the Juniors."

A gasp all round! Another gasp when they realised this was true. The real Pymble.

Suddenly everyone realised that this boy could sing—because

he really could sing! He was famous; a star, and nobody had noticed. Endless cheering filled the space to everyone's enjoyment, when Margaret suddenly said,

"Has anybody seen Mrs Lorelei?"

CHAPTER 17.
STARS IN THEIR EYES

THE TEAM WERE ALREADY SOLIDLY underway with preparations for the next stage. All the equipment could be easily taken through The Bali Ahoy Senior Social Club to the beach just below. The quantity of goods was still a bit off-putting, though. Nobody, not even Ek, had any idea how many survivors were still in the waters of Blue-Green Planet, nor in what medical and emotional condition they would be found. They had all been through so much. It was particularly upsetting to the Westall crew to contemplate this thought. They were just ordinary kids from ordinary families who took the difficulties of life in their stride, and of course they had all faced difficulties at one time or another, but to be hurled into a Salty Pot in another world with a likely future of being torn apart and eaten, well this was beyond them all. They could only busy themselves with the preparations and be as organised and efficient as they could for when the time came. Sometimes, waiting for 'the time' to come is a painful eternity in itself, even though nothing actually happens, and the students felt this isolation deeply.

Margaret and Pymble had gathered up all the cactus stems that had proved to be such an effective prop in the floor show, and they headed off to the flower shop to return them.

"Isn't this just about the best school day we've ever had?" asked Margaret.

"Certainly is," replied Pymble. "One thing though."

"Something missing, isn't there?"

"Yeah, that's what I thought, too."

"He's the one who stood up for everyone."

"Yeah, and he knew the Alien Craft was real."

"And then all the bullying they threw at him."

"You know what we have to do, don't you?"

"Let's go, Pymble!"

They ran off with enthusiasm and vigour, looking for Inspector Ash Pendale and his sergeant to give them a bit of a hand of the transport variety.

***

The whirring rotors of the helicopter seemed to suddenly take on an extra surge of energy.

"There's something handy about helicopters, Mum: shortcuts!"

"Tell me about it, Bobby, those two suckers have been chugging around the Bay forever. They think they've pulled a swifty, coming around the whole of the Bay."

"Nobody takes Team Chow Palace for a ride, Mum!"

"Too right! But maybe we should take them for a bit of a spin. Where exactly are we, Bobby?"

"Mum! A pilot isn't supposed to ask that! Anyway, we're just offshore from Dromana."

"Perfect timing. Can you see them coming yet?"

"Yep, a few shakes of a lamb's tale and they'll be smack over the Dromana foreshore. I'll call in the other fifty helicopters to act as a dramatic backdrop behind us. Never waste a moment. How about a few swoops first?"

"Ah, we think alike, as always. OK, I can see them. Me first, then you."

Auntie could operate the helicopter like it was like a small doorknob. She directed the whirring machine along the same altitude they had been on in their tours of the bay while they waited for their prey. Down below, Dullard and Stipple had no idea that they were doomed, like rabbits stalked by a powerful eagle. The only difference was these two rabbits weren't little, fluffy or harmless. They had caused more hurt and grief than anyone could reasonably remember—until now.

"Co-pilot to Pilot," yelled Auntie, "Cliff-Top Manoeuvre. Go! Go! Go!"

As if the helicopter itself had ears, its path took an immediate ninety degree turn to the ground.

"Wee! Wee!" exploded Auntie, who loved acrobatics, aerobatics

Westall '66 The Final Truth

and astrobatics, which was the sense of feeling really dizzy if you went too far with the first two.

"Regulate to Scalp Manoeuvre," squealed Bobby, and the chopper levelled itself, equal to the ground, but zooming only millimetres above the heads of Stipple and Dullard, who started screaming hysterically at the reality of this massive machine shearing overhead, literally.

"Reverse Scalp Flat Top!" ordered Auntie, who was beside herself as the co-star of this fairground attraction. At once, the precision machine turned and set upon the motorcycle twins once more, this time mowing their hairstyles to the barest minimum.

"Reach for the Stars," urged Bobby as he pulled the throttle to guide the helicopter to its highest point in the sky. "Activate the hook." Beneath them they could hear the clunking of a solid hook on the end of a solid chain.

"All right, Bobby, this is it. Go reel them in." They were, of course, more than aware that the chorus of fifty extra helicopters was now in place above them, imitating every move they made.

The swooping eagle once more descended, and when it was close enough, Bobby made sure the hook was clasped around the handlebars of the motorbike. When he was sure he had made a connection, he quickly raised the helicopter back into the sky, with the motorbike hanging limp and powerless below. Stipple and Dullard were clearly beside themselves, screaming, weeping, accusing each other; everything that any reasonable person would expect from nasty, vicious bullies like these two.

"Activate Washing Machine Manoeuvre!"

This was the Grand Finale; slowly, slowly, the helicopter started circling around itself, then, like a dazzling ice skater, the circles became faster and faster. The motorbike was now flying around with the helicopter, at the same height. The fifty helicopters above them spun with equal vigour. The trick had the effect of looking at a fairground ride, and this was mother and son's absolute favourite.

"Reel them in," shouted Bobby, "it's time to go home, kiddies." The circles slowed down, then with one disciplined swoop, the helicopter swept in the direction of Mount Eliza. They spotted some action outside what looked like a clubhouse, and recognised some of their fellow travellers. Carefully, they eased the helicopter just low enough so that the motorbike was suspended just half a centimetre above ground level.

"We're back from our fishing trip, me and Mum. Police help needed," Bobby said.

Inspector Pendale didn't need to be told twice, and luckily the Constables who had taken the old people had just returned from The Morning Star Home for Bad Boys.

"Leave them to me, son," the inspector said into his megaphone, "we've got 'em! Just park your chopper by the road there. Come on men, unclip these two and take them to Morning Star with the others."

Just before Bobby and Auntie said goodnight to their helicopter, they quickly wound down the windows and waved to the adoring crowd below. A huge cheer of approval bounced across the water, endlessly encouraging, endlessly supportive of all. It was very kind of that helicopter Pilot, Lieutenant Porter, to lend his chopper to Auntie and Bobby for a bit. But then again, it was in exchange for a free meal at The Chow Palace, once a week for five years.

***

The transfer of all materials needed for the care of the Oktopi trapped in the waters of what was now known to be Port Phillip Bay had only barely begun when Bobby and Mum/Auntie slid into view with their victory landing. There was still so much to be done before anyone could even think of any subsequent stages.

In essence, the whole of Bali Ahoy Beach had to be converted into a working Beach Hospital. The Oktopi would need to be transferred from the water to dry land, then examined and tested, treated and tended, and nurtured until a move could be made. This required so many skills, and who had them?

The necessary supplies and equipment were being sorted on the sand. Sheila and Kayleen organised what should go where. They seemed to have a natural sense of the order that the processes would take, and on the sand they created little 'wards', with beds made from the plastic containers.

Apart from the care of the Oktopi, Con also realised that they, the students, needed to be cared for as well. He addressed the workers, saying, "I've looked inside The Club, and there's plenty of food and drink, but we're going to need a couple of chefs as well to take care of our catering needs as well. Anyone interested?"

Out of the blue, two hands shot up. "We will, Con, no worries," shouted back Coles and Ray. "Glad to help!" They headed back inside to see how they could manage things.

The whole time, I stood by, fascinated by the endless teamwork that everyone contributed to. Every classmate had ability in something, but together, like this, was an awesome, powerful group to be with. They had found the power of the octopus.

What's more, thanks to them, I'd found it too.

"Also, we need a doctor to coordinate everything we do. If you think this is for you, just come and see me."

For quite a few minutes, there was no response. Then Con heard behind him, "I think I'd like to do that, Con." Con swung around and there was William, smiling calmly and confidently.

"William, I couldn't imagine a better bloke for the job."

Together they walked back to the field hospital. William seemed to know exactly what to do. He rearranged just about everything there was to rearrange and ordered the cleaning of every smallest instrument, but nobody minded because he was, after all, William.

"Right. One small request please," he said in his calm, dignified voice, "more specific help is needed. Two excellent swimmers. Do we have these? It's a vital job."

"Oksana's the school swimming champion," said sister Umame, "you don't get better than that." Oksana waved to William to indicate she'd happily swim.

"I'll do it." It was Mr Bleach. Then he smiled and said,"I'm probably the second-fastest swimmer in the school."

"Done, but now we're going to figure out some sort of transport by sea," said William. He was about to add something, but the roar of engines stopped him mid breath. The roar continued to grow, but the cause was quite unclear because all lights out there had been turned off. One by one the engines were cut, then all at once a bright beam lit up the vision—twenty or so navy vessels, with the front one showing a special feature. On the front bow stood Mrs Mavis Lorelei, and just at the right moment she called out, "Ini and Itu!"

An explosive, "ini" and "itu" greeted her back, twenty, fifty, one hundred times. Goodness knows where or how she managed to get all these ships. "Well don't just hang about; my brother said we can use these tubs for one night, and one night only!"

"What do you mean, 'your brother'? Why does he own twenty ships?"

"Because he's the Admiral of the Australian Navy, of course. But there's no war on at the moment or anything like that, so we're in luck." Mrs Lorelei beamed from ear to ear.

"Mrs Lorelei, this is what we'll do," said William, "our swim-mers will collect one Oktopus at a time from the sea. They will hand these to you. You allocate which ship they will go on, and that ship will bring them to the jetty here. You have plenty of ships with you to rotate as a round-robin. We have swimmers of the highest standard. There will be medical staff on the jetty and so on. We are so grateful to all of you. Right, are the swimmers ready?" Oksana and Mr Bleach emerged from the Clubhouse where they had managed to find some swimwear. Oksana had some frilly clown-like neck to knees thing, but Mr Bleach could only find the largest bathers ever created, and he'd made these fit by tying about twenty knots in them. They had both come to the conclusion that it was all for a good cause.

"Right, swimmers ready?"

"Ready!"

"Ships ready?"

"Ready!"

"Jetty staff ready?"

"Ready!"

"Hospital staff ready?"

"Ready!"

"Supplies staff ready?"

"Ready!"

"Ready Ready?"

"Ready!"

"Thank you, William, and everyone. I will soon be making contact with my people from the Outer Galaxy," I said, excited that we'd all come so far in this mission. "That will, of course be the final destination for the poor creatures, my people, that we are here to help. Oksana and Mr Bleach, you may start your swim ... now!"

Off they went, in a sea that was becoming increasingly choppy. Then, just like that they were gone, out of sight, searching for the colony or even colonies that could be living in, or even beyond this bay. Some nervous minutes passed, and quite a few of us were having feelings of some concern. How far did they have to swim, and how deep?

As suddenly as the two had vanished underwater, they reappeared gasping for air, but each holding an Oktopus. Each Oktopus clung gratefully, but pathetically onto one arm of its saviour. A quick transfer to the ship, and the trail was on. Scout saw the urgent need and joined the swimming team. Berenice approached William and told him that, while she wasn't a flash swimmer like the others, she would offer to check out how many would have to be evacuated. That well-oiled machine was on a roll again.

I separated myself from the others for a bit to try and activate my contact with Mother. I had forgotten that I didn't have my panel any more. I tried several mental connections that I knew could work under certain conditions, like a snowstorm or an avalanche of lights, but since these weren't apparent, I wasn't getting very far. A sudden light came up at me from the sand, and it read, "ALREADY ACTIVATED COMMANDER BLUE-GREEN". I felt I had no other choice but to believe its message, so I returned to The Hospital where I could not believe my eyes. In my short absence, The Hospital had turned into a beehive of activity. Hundreds of Oktopi had already been rescued. I ran into Berenice and asked how many were still down in the water, and she said there were thousands. William said there were plenty of supplies, but it was quite stressful for the staff, because so many of the Oktopi were clearly tearful and scared. I knew immediately what I had to do. I morphed out of my Blue-Green Planet clothes, and I was back as myself, as Prince Ek. I went from little plastic tub to the next, talking to each poor victim about all the cruelties they had seen and endured. I promised them my strength and care, and also the strength of all the young people around me. I sat and held an arm as comfort, as friendship. I loved them. I had to keep moving, too exhausted to share my time with them all. There were so many, too many, but I struggled on; we all did, until every last one had been taken from the water. All were safe; the last few were now being bundled and ready for travel.

"Thank you, everyone, thank you for all you have done."

"You're just brilliant, Ek," said Con, "sure you can't stay at Westall?"

"Westall already has a prince, Con. You."

"You know what, Ek, all this has really been our pleasure," said Auntie, who had been gently massaging the many, many Arms. "We don't put up with crap on this planet."

"Something nice to eat, Ek? Con? Auntie?"

It was Coles, and he and Ray had been busy slaving over a hot oven to produce some nice snacks for all the workers. There were trays full of cakes, biscuits, tarts, eclairs, veggie pasties, sultana pies, tomatoes stuffed with mayonnaise, peppers stuffed with mustard, and mustard and pepper stuffed with tomato sauce. It was a veritable feast, and I gladly enjoyed what the boys called their Pineapple and Chilli Boat.

"This is amazing food, guys, well done," I said, meaning every mouthful.

"Excellent, boys," said Auntie. "I wonder if you'd like to come over to the Chow Palace one night, and help us with a new menu. We've got to think ahead into the 70s, you know."

It was like a giant zip had suddenly ripped through the sky. Flaps of black fell to the sides, increasing the curtain of gold and red that now appeared in their place. What started as tiny specks of deepest blue grew larger and larger until the sky before us was filled with rapidly descending Oktokrafts, a hundred in all. They landed on the water and around the ships, quietly so as not to disturb the many patients lying in our hospital on the sand.

Mother's Oktokraft was at the front; I could see the Royal Insignia beaming. The exit shaft slid open, and she came out.

209

She looked concerned, troubled, but I kept my distance just in case. From her small handbag, she produced a little box, which she unfolded to create a tiny chair to sit on.

"Thank you for receiving us, people of Blue-Green Planet. Forgive the invasion, but so many people wanted to come with me today. Ek, my son, our journey together here was so difficult. I have had time to think, and I want to tell you what you should know."

There was a complete hush over the beach. This woman had such stature, such control and inner power. This was the impression she cast on the crowd, and even from her little stool, everyone could hear her words, clear as a bell. Ek had to admit there was a bit of a difference between this mother and the one he last saw in The Grange.

"Ek, I have something to tell you that is of the gravest importance. When you were born, Ek, you were not alone. You were one of twins, and you had a twin sister. My two beautiful, perfect babies. Ek and Eek, that was your sister's name. One day, and I can still only barely bring myself to say it, your sister Eek went missing. She disappeared. I blamed myself, endlessly, to such an extent I could think of nothing else. Self-blame, self-blame. That became my whole reason for living. Your father, King Ok, focussed entirely on you, Ek, as a way of coping. In his mind, you could do no wrong: 'Ek's so cute, clever, funny, helpful, kind, creative, strong.' It was wrong, so very wrong, Ek, but I started to take things out on you. I made up all sorts of reasons why you were supposedly useless, selfish, weak, unkind, uncaring and so on, but I couldn't stop, just as King Ok couldn't stop singing your praises. I just wanted my baby back, my family back, and so did he."

I could see a tear flow from one eye. She was in a tragic, lonely agony.

"And now, here we are. I've been watching you, Ek, the natural leader that you are, taking such good care of these children here, and organising the safe release of our fellow Oktopi to come home at last. Ek, I've treated you like you don't exist, because I've been so afraid to lose you too." She cried again, this time so intensely that it was almost frightening. I felt I had to do something significant.

There she was sitting on that little stool, so alone, so broken. I walked up to her and gently tapped her on the shoulder. She looked up slowly, and I softly said,

"Move over, Fatty."

It was the right thing. She pulled me down next to her and grabbed me in one of those forever hugs that more than made up for those years of living with 'horror Mum'.

"I'm so sorry, Ek."

"Me too."

"What for? What did you do?"

"I should've called you Fatty earlier."

For the first time, we laughed; a laugh that lit up every byway and celestial back road of every known galaxy and quite a few unknown ones as well.

"Mum, can I ask you a question? Can I have your last packet of Colour Change Powder Pickle?"

And she ran off, laughing, shouting, and then she devoured the whole thing herself. Or at least she seemed to. When I approached, she produced the whole packet intact and full.

"Presto, Ek. Enjoy!"

"No! We'll all be poisoned! Thanks for the thought, Mum. Oh, one more strange question though. I wasn't able to activate the Panel today to call you."

"That's odd, because it had already been activated."

"But from where?"

"This planet."

There was a point of thinking here. Where was it that I had seen a shimmer in front of my eyes—the sort of shimmer that could only have come from one of our own people. At the time, we had all been too busy sorting out our immediate problems, but now, some investigation might lead to a solution. I called Maya.

"Maya, I'd like you to meet my mum, Queen Aggratenta. Maya, when you saw me leave the Oktokraft back in the Grange, and you saw 'half Oktopus me' morphing into schoolboy Ek, was there anybody else there that you saw?"

Maya shuffled around for a bit and said, "Yes, I saw another Oktopus. A very kind one. She tried to help me but all of a sudden there were too many people all around, and then you had disappeared, Ek, and she had too."

"This is most odd, Ek," said Mum, "Who in the Galaxies could this have been?"

From right behind her, a voice said, "It was me, Mum."

From sheer terror to love, Mum swung around to be face to face with what she thought could never be possible. "Oh Eek, my daughter, my baby daughter, whatever happened to you?" Mum began to break down as the reality of their reunion hit her. All three of us were caught between needing to know what had happened, and simply needing to hold each other forever, so we would never be separated again, a triangle of lost and found without understanding the rules.

Eek said, "At the time when the KruiseKraft was about to depart, which ended up here in such a terrible state of disaster, I had been playing just inside the entrance. I didn't even notice the latch slide shut and we were off before I even knew it. I've been here ever since, and I saw no hope of ever seeing you again until Ek landed, a bit abruptly perhaps, at The Grange. There's one more thing. Here is Ek's Panel. I took it from The Grange. That's how I was able to contact you."

Mum just stood and sobbed, that agonised sobbing that only a parent can feel in the most intimate moments of parental happiness or pain. We went and stood on either side of her, and we hugged for a blissful eternity, all twenty-four Arms entwined. There are times when eight Arms each are an absolute bonus.

Both communities watched in disbelief that such a reunion could have occurred. Finally, Mum spoke again, but this time as Queen Aggratenta.

"All those who are gathered here now, please heed my words. On this day, let it be known that I bring a most updated message on behalf of King Ok, my husband, and myself. King Ok and I have spent many Okts as proud rulers of ULTERIATA BLACK HOLE GALAXY SUPERMASSIVATA. We have loved our nation and our citizens. We are now at the stage when our community would be better served by rulers who are not wracked by old age as we are now. We had not been certain who should succeed our Royal selves, but the decision has now been made. The future rulers of our vast nation will be my children, those we all see before us. Ek and Eek. Arise King Ek and Queen Eek."

I think Eek was probably as gobsmacked as I was.

"Mum, you have about seventy other children to choose from, and we're the youngest!"

"Rubbish," she replied, "the two of you have experienced more trauma than all the others combined, you have both shown greater qualities of care, and sensitivity and responsibility, and you have both worked towards this most remarkable day, without ever knowing it would occur. You, King Ek and Queen Eek, are now the rightful Monarchs of our Dominions."

Everyone stood in quiet respect, realising they were witness to a great Intergalactic moment.

Only Mr Bleach moved; he walked towards us.

"May I suggest, Noble King and Queen, that you might find it desirable to accompany yourselves with an advisor, a mentor, a guide to help you, especially since such an individual might already be known to you."

He faced them solidly; bit by bit and to the shock of the Royals, the familiar Mr Bleach faded away to a shimmering, loved and respected member of their society.

I beamed a huge smile. "Well, well, Mr Bleach, you're not Mr Bleach at all. You're cousin Each!"

"That's right, Ek. I was on the original KruiseKraft too, on a holiday. Well, fine holiday it turned out to be. Anyway, I quickly realised Eek was on board by mistake, so I made it my business to look after her. Then the dreadful accident happened. I knew we had to get out of harm's way, so I found a small pool for us, just underneath the Bali Ahoy Senior Social Club. There was always so much food wastage from those ancient ones, vegetarian waste at that, that we always had plenty to eat. It just seemed to dribble and crumble non-stop. Just goes to show it takes more than a vegetable to make a good person. Anyway, I saw your Oktokraft soaring overhead, so in desperation combined with excitement, I morphed myself into Mr Bleach and shaped him into the local Time and Reality Zones. The rest you know, and I must say, Ek … I mean, King Ek … you've been amazing!"

"I couldn't have done it without you, Bleach … Each. I thought you were the kindest on this planet—apart from William maybe."

A small but significant procession headed towards The Royal Family. "Coles and Ray have organised this gift," said Margaret, as she and Pymble ushered a walking parcel wrapped up in a special kind of glittering seaweed. The party was led by Mr Glass, and supported by a cavalcade of police motorcyclists who had provided the transport.

"Excuse me," he said quietly.

"Don't tell me you are an Oktopus too," laughed Mum.

"Dear me, no," replied Mr Glass, "I don't actually know what star sign I am, but I do have a major announcement to make. I realise that, while my life was made unbearably difficult by those two whose names I don't wish to speak, I do think in my heart of hearts I should have tried harder to regain some sense of peace and stability in the school, but I just didn't know how to do this, and I will be forever sorry. I have resigned from my position, and this gives me a great sense of calm. Now I wish to introduce my replacement, the new Headmaster of Westall High School."

Margaret and Pymble guided the walking seaweed up to the front, accompanied by the two police officers who had provided the transport, complete with sirens. With a small flick, they removed the seaweed wrapping, and at the same time Mr Glass announced, "Mr Ollie Gently!"

A huge, huge roar rose up, to be heard for at least 37 Okts in any direction. This was justice whichever way you looked at it. Mr Gently was a gifted man of humanity, with an understanding of what mattered to people.

Mum tapped me on my back, "Ek, what's a Headmaster?"

"It's a King, Mum, this man's a real Blue-Green Planet King."

Mr Gently signalled that he wished to speak. "Thank you everyone, so very much. However, this is not about me. I've had a quick chat with William, and he's anxious that we should start moving our OktoPatients into the Krafts to get them home. Mr Bleach, would it be possible, if we were all to accompany your party back to your home, that you could adjust the time zones so when we do get back, nobody will even notice we've been gone?"

Another great cheer went up. Talk about holidays overseas; this sounded even better than Phillip Island.

Bleach looked like he was in deep thought. Of course he wasn't, as he is part of the family after all. At last he looked up and said intelligently, "Too easy!"

The moving of the many patients was handled as efficiently as their retrieval from the sea. Further help came from the Oktopi from all the Kraft. Of course, everything could have fitted in the one Oktokraft, but this was a Grand Event of the Grandest Nature, and it was fine reason for a great display and celebration.

With everything almost packed ready for departure, Inspector Pendale walked up to me and offered his hand.

"Thank you, Inspector, you have been incredible."

"Bewdy, son," answered Pendale, as we shook hands.

I took one final look at the beach, recalling my whole time with these kids from a little school on a little planet. Something caught my attention, on the sand, but indistinct in the darkness. I approached it and saw it was a solid poster of some kind, in bright red and gold. I suddenly realised it was that sign from The Chow Palace, and how human and equal I felt when Bobby had made fun of me.

I picked up the sign and put it under my Arms. I laughed. I was going to take it home as a fine present for Father Ok. He'd enjoy the joke too.

I entered the Oktokraft and slowly activated the Close Panel Activation. I requested that all Oktokrafts do one more last thing, and, before we sped back into deep space, we embarked on a slow and dignified Lap of Honour around Westall High School. I picked up the Soundboks, and after a short reflection, I addressed all.

"Thank you, it's been a great day. A couple of thoughts though before I mount The Royal Konsole. First, I don't think I can allow my mother to go through life with a name like Aggratenta any longer. So from today, she will be called … Nicole, the Queen Mother.

Second, let it be known that wherever the names of King Ek and Queen Eek are spoken, the following must be obeyed:

'In the Dominions spanning from ULTERIATA BLACK HOLE GALAXY SUPERMASSIVATA to Westall High School, all citizens from the smallest dot infant to the most ancient frail being, shall, no matter what, enjoy the Human and Oktopine qualities of thriving, learning, creating, nurturing and expressing, in environments that treasure and protect these. Any breach of these rights will be harshly regarded by all, but acted upon specifically by Bobby and his Mum.' I wish you well. Remember, the best leadership comes from enabling others to lead themselves."

Bobby turned to everyone, "Hey Mum, guys, anybody want to try a Wagon Wheel? I've still got a few!

AUTHOR'S NOTE

We are obsessed with the ideas of leadership and control. Tragic really, since we're already born with these qualities. We just have to apply them as needed. This is what the Westall High School kids did so effectively in 1966.

Made in the USA
Middletown, DE
26 June 2022

67850087R00139